A Long Pitch Home

A Long Pitch Home

Natalie Dias Lorenzi

◖◗ Charlesbridge

To the new kids in class, and to those who befriend them.

First paperback edition 2018
Text copyright © 2016 by Natalie Dias Lorenzi
Illustrations copyright © 2016 by Kelly Murphy

Published by Charlesbridge
85 Main Street
Watertown, MA 02472
(617) 926-0329
www.charlesbridge.com

Library of Congress Cataloging-in-Publication Data
Names: Lorenzi, Natalie Dias, author.
A long pitch home / by Natalie Dias Lorenzi.
Watertown, MA : Charlesbridge, [2016] | Summary: When Bilal's family suddenly moves to
    America, his father stays in Pakistan, and Bilal embraces baseball, an unexpected friend,
    and a new language. But this new way of life does not feel so special without Baba—
    will he ever get to America to see Bilal pitch a game?
Identifiers: LCCN 2015026830 | ISBN 9781580897136 (reinforced for library use)
    | ISBN 9781580898263 (softcover)
    | ISBN 9781607348702 (ebook)
    | ISBN 9781607348719 (ebook pdf)
Subjects: LCSH: Pakistanis—United States—Juvenile fiction. | Pakistani Americans—
    Juvenile fiction. | Families—Juvenile fiction. | Culture shock—Juvenile fiction. | Cousins—
    Juvenile fiction.| Fathers and sons—Juvenile fiction. | CYAC: Pakistanis—United States—
    Fiction. | Pakistani Americans—Fiction. | Muslims—Fiction. | Family life—Fiction.|
    Culture shock—Fiction. | Cousins—Fiction. | Fathers and sons—Fiction. | Baseball—
    Fiction.
Classification: LCC PZ7.L885 So 2016 | DDC [Fic]—dc23
    LC record available at http://lccn.loc.gov/2015026830

Printed in the United States of America
(hc) 10 9 8 7 6 5 4 3 2 1
(sc) 10 9 8 7 6 5 4 3 2 1

Display type set in Paquita Pro by Juanjo Lopez
Text type set in Adobe Caslon Pro by Adobe Systems Incorporated
Color separations by Coral Graphic Services, Inc., in Hicksville, New York, USA
Printed by Berryville Graphics in Berryville, Virginia, USA
Production supervision by Brian G. Walker
Designed by Diane M. Earley

 # One

They took my father three days ago, a week before my tenth birthday.

No one knows where he is. Or if they do know, they are not telling me.

Daddo has her own theories. "They took my son because he is the best engineer in all of Karachi—no, in all of Pakistan."

"Who are *they*?" I ask.

My grandmother frowns as she strips the mango skin from its flesh. I actually feel sorry for the mango.

She does not answer my question, so I keep talking.

"But Daddo, there are a thousand engineers in Karachi. Why couldn't they—whoever *they* are—get their own engineer instead of taking Baba?"

"Bah." Daddo scoops up the mango peels and dumps them in the trash. "You are still too young to understand these things, Bilal."

"Almost-ten-year-olds are not too young to understand these things."

I hold my breath, waiting for her reaction. I am not supposed to be disrespectful during the month of Ramadan. Or any of the other months, either.

But Daddo doesn't look mad. She just shakes her head and says, "One day you will understand."

Here is what I understand.

Four days ago I was planning my birthday party with my mother. Ammi called the Pie in the Sky bakery over by Zamzama Park and ordered my favorite cake—chocolate malt with fudge frosting.

The next day my father never came home from work.

I understand nothing.

Ammi has not cooked a thing since my father disappeared. Daddo cooks double of everything to feed the relatives who stream into our apartment every day, waiting for news about my father.

Usually my family is loud, and we talk all at once except when we're laughing. But whoever took my father took our laughter, too. The grown-ups smile whenever I come into the room with my little sister, Hira, who hasn't let me out of her sight since our father disappeared. They clap whenever Humza, my baby brother, toddles over and calls out a nonsense word. But I can see in their eyes that they are scared. Their fear sits on my chest like an elephant.

The adults gather in the living room, where the curtains are drawn against the late-afternoon sun. They stop whispering when I come around the corner, so I catch only snippets of their conversations.

"He should have transferred out of that office."

"How many times did I tell him not to push the issue?"

"I've never trusted Tahir."

I understand none of it, especially the part about Tahir, the father of my very best friend. He and Baba work together. They have been friends since they were boys, just like Mudassar and me.

When the sun sinks into the sea and the *azaan* sounds from the minarets of the Mubarak Mosque, our prayers do not feel joyful. I kneel on my *janamaz*, touching my forehead to the prayer mat. But when I recite the traditional words, I am really asking Allah to bring Baba home. When it is time to break the fast, no one rushes to the table; they shuffle and murmur and sigh. Daddo brings out the steaming bowls of *qorma*, and the smell of chicken and curry makes my stomach rumble. I feel guilty for being hungry, because who knows if those people who took Baba are letting him eat. Daddo must hear my rumbling belly, because she leans over as she passes the plate of dates and whispers, "Eat, Bilal *jaan*. Worrying is hungry work."

We mumble an unenthusiastic *Bismillah* in thanks for our food. Maybe Allah heard our prayer, because next we hear the knock at the door. Everyone freezes except for Humza, who stuffs his mouth with fat fistfuls of mushy rice and peas.

Nobody moves because that first knock is just a regular one. But then it comes, Baba's special knock: two fast raps— pause—another quick knock like a hiccup, followed by two solid thunks.

We burst from our chairs in a blur of movement, our voices exploding with hope and disbelief. Someone's water glass clanks over and my chair crashes to the floor, but I do not look back. My legs race down the hall until my palms slam against the front door.

My fingers work the locks as fast as dragonfly wings, and then—*click!*—the last of the locks is free. I pull the door open, and there stands Baba. His suit is wrinkled and his shirt is torn near the pocket, and he must have lost his glasses somewhere along the way. But it's him, all right, and he is home.

"Baba!" I yell. My father smiles and steps inside, then falls to his knees and opens his arms. Hira and I just about knock him over. His cheek has the beginnings of a beard that prickles my own cheek, but I keep my arms tight around him. Everyone surrounds my father, crying and laughing and asking him where he's been. He only shakes his head and takes turns holding us close.

Baba doesn't speak about those three days he was missing from our lives. But two days after his surprise homecoming, he says this: "Bilal, it is high time we leave Pakistan to live with your Hassan Uncle and Noor Auntie in America."

America? That's on the other side of the world.

Ammi, my siblings, and I will leave in a few days, and Baba will come later. In the meantime, Baba says we can tell no one we are leaving, not even Mudassar. Especially not Mudassar. If Baba and Tahir are no longer friends, does that mean I have lost my best friend, too?

✦   ✦   ✦

We have two days to pack our things. Not all of our things: only one suitcase each. How can a person fit his whole life into one suitcase? It is impossible. Ammi says it is hard to decide what to take because we have so many nice things, and for that we should be thankful. But I am not thankful I have to leave my cricket bat behind—the one my teammates signed after we won last season's Karachi Youth Tournament. I do take my cricket uniform and the photo of Mudassar and me grinning after our final win. I unpin another photo—the one of Baba when he played on Pakistan's national team. I run my finger along the row of famous faces sitting near Baba—left-arm bowler Waqas Akram, and the team captain, the great Omar Khan. The picture was taken right before Baba injured his knee and couldn't play in the World Cup. It was the last season he ever played.

The only thing left on my bulletin board is the ticket stub from the Karachi Zebras versus the Peshawar Panthers match—the very first cricket match Baba took me to see. The ticket stub is wedged between the cork and the bulletin board's frame, and I have to tug a few times to get it out. I leave my cricket helmet. There is so much I cannot take.

Still, I fill my suitcase to bursting, and now our last day in Karachi is here. We are standing in the Jinnah International Airport on July the fourth at four o'clock in the morning. My *baba* tells me this: "Today will be the best day of your life, Bilal."

I do not say anything, because I am too busy wondering what my father will tell my friends tomorrow afternoon when they come to our door expecting to celebrate my birthday, arms full of presents. I am thinking about how my chocolate malt cake with fudge frosting will be sitting in the refrigerator in the back of the Pie in the Sky bakery. When the baker figures out no one is coming to get my cake, maybe he will take it home to his own family for their Eid celebration at the end of Ramadan.

My father leans down to look me in the eye, and I blink hard. "Bilal," he says, "cricket has taught you strength and resilience. To do your best even when things are not easy. To support your teammates." He swallows, and I wonder if his throat feels tight like mine does. Baba's eyes don't leave mine, and his voice is firm when he tells me, "Now it is time to be strong for your mother, your sister, and your brother."

Losing a cricket match after trying your best for five hours is not the same as moving to America. I do not say this to Baba. Instead I take a shaky breath and blink fast to keep my tears from spilling down my cheeks.

"You will see, Bilal," he says, his voice gentler now. "Today is the beginning of a new life for us. Not only is today your birthday, but—guess what?" He smiles. "It is America's birthday, too."

I nod like this is good news, but how can today be the best day of my life if we are leaving Baba behind? I would give up birthday parties for the rest of my life if only he could come with us now.

Hira tugs on my father's sleeve. "Baba, why can't you come to America now, with us?"

"I have to take care of some things at work, *baytee*." He takes Hira's hand. "Your uncle will be there to meet you, and I will come as soon as I can. Do not worry."

I worry anyway.

Humza chews on a cookie as he watches a cart loaded with suitcases roll past. He has no idea we will not see Baba for who knows how long. He has no idea he's supposed to feel sad. I wish I could trade places with him. My father kisses the top of Humza's head before pulling Hira and me into one last hug. Then he holds my mother close. She cries enough silent tears to fill the Lyari River. Hira slips her hand into mine, and I gently squeeze it. She is only six. I will be ten by the time this day is over—too old to cry in front of my father. When my mother finally pulls herself from Baba's arms, we walk under the Unaccompanied Women and Children sign for the first time in our lives and head toward the desk where a man is checking passports. He stifles a yawn as he stamps our papers.

When we are through the line, my mother says to look straight ahead and be strong.

I don't listen. At the last moment, I turn and see Baba, his hand over his mouth and his eyes full of pain. When he sees me, he puts a kiss into that hand and sends it my way. I catch it, like I always do, and pat it onto my heart extra hard, so it will stick. My eyes sting, blurring my last look at Baba before I run to catch up to my mother.

When the plane finally lifts us into the air, I realize I never sent Baba a kiss back. I send one now into the shadows of the sunrise and hope it will travel through the airplane window and find its way to him.

"He will join us soon, Bilal. You will see."

I nod, still looking out the window as Karachi shrinks into a toy city with blinking lights. *He will join us soon.* I repeat my mother's words in my head over and over, because I want to believe they are true.

My father said that today, the fourth of July, would be the best day of my life. My father is wrong.

 TWO

The very first thing Uncle says to me at the airport is, "Happy birthday, Bilal! I can't believe you are already nine." I know why he can't believe I am nine; it is because I am ten. But I do not tell this to Uncle. I think he would be embarrassed not to know the age of his only sister's son, even though the last time I saw him was back when I was in Class 1, barely six years old. That was just before Uncle moved his family to America, and we stayed in Karachi.

We follow Uncle out to a huge car that he calls *mini*—a minivan. The air feels like Karachi—warm and thick—but the sounds here are different. As we load our suitcases into the van, not one horn honks in this whole gigantic parking lot. It looks funny to see Uncle sitting behind the steering wheel on the left side of the car and Ammi sitting next to him, where the steering wheel should be. When we start to drive, I can see why Uncle is sitting on the wrong side: everyone drives on the wrong side of the road instead of the left.

Hira peppers Uncle with questions the whole way, but her voice eventually fades from my ears as I take in the scenery rolling past the window.

We zoom along a wide road with four neat lanes. It's nothing like Karachi, where sometimes you can't tell which lane is which because scooters weave between cars, minibuses chug alongside men on bikes, and donkeys pull carts carrying bricks or boxes or sacks of food. The few buses on this American road all look exactly the same; not a single one is decorated with colorful designs, and no fringe hangs from their bumpers. No one rides on top or hangs out of the doors or windows.

Uncle turns into his neighborhood, where the houses are like the cars on the highway—neatly spaced, very big, and mostly the same. I don't see any palm trees, just leafy giants as tall as our apartment building back in Karachi. Each house has its own garden right out front, and most of the cars are parked on small lanes that lead to garages. The one car parked in the wide street is yellow with a rounded roof and hubcaps that look like white flower petals.

Uncle parks in his own lane in front of his garage and says, "Here we are!"

Hira gasps. "This is your *house*, Mamoo?"

Uncle laughs. "It is your house, too, Hira *jaan!*"

Looking at the brick front and six windows of the two-story house, I can't believe only three people live here. Well, now it will be seven. Eight when Baba comes.

Ammi takes in a breath. "What a lovely house, *Bhai jaan!*"

Uncle presses a button that opens the back of the van. "Thank you, *Baji*."

It is strange to hear my mother call someone *brother* and to hear her called *sister*. I think of her only as Ammi.

We step through the front door, passing a staircase and a living room on the left. Down a hall there is another living room with a brick fireplace, and then a kitchen so big that there are two places to sit—at a round table with six chairs and a high chair for Humza, or on tall stools around a square counter in the center of the kitchen.

The very first thing Auntie says when she greets us is, "Bilal! You must be hungry." I have always liked Auntie. She looks exactly the same as I remember. When I tell her so, she gives me an extra hug.

Behind her I see yet another room off the kitchen with a fancy table and chairs.

The front door slams and in jogs Jalaal, who towers over Auntie. The very first thing my cousin says to me is, "Hey, little buddy."

I do not know this English word *buddy*, but I know *little*. Does he think I am so little? Maybe he also thinks I am still nine. Then he slides his hands into his American jeans pockets and switches from English to Urdu to say his second thing, which is this: "Don't worry—I'll teach you everything you need to know about living in America."

I believe him, because he speaks Urdu with an American accent. Then he switches back to English. "Your mom says you're pretty good with English."

I shrug and smile. "I like learning the new word," I answer, so Jalaal can hear for himself.

Jalaal nods. "Nice." He picks up my backpack and switches back to Urdu. "Come on, I'll show you where to put your stuff."

Hira takes my hand. "I want to come, too."

We follow Jalaal up the stairs. Having steps inside the house feels like living in two apartments all at once. Our building in Karachi has a stairwell that goes up all twelve stories, but we only use it when the power is out and the elevator doesn't run.

Jalaal leads us down the hallway. "This is my parents' room." He points through double doors to a room with a bed our whole family could probably fit on. We pass another room. "That's where your mom will stay." A crib for Humza sits next to a double bed that must be for Hira and my mom. But then Jalaal points to yet another door and says, "Hira, this is your room."

"Oh!" She claps in delight and pushes the door all the way open. Light pink walls match the pillows on the bed. A stuffed bear sits on a rocking chair, and Hira's name is spelled out in white letters on one wall.

"Do you like it?" Jalaal waves his hand across the room like a showman. "I painted the walls. I heard you like pink."

Hira beams and throws her arms around Jalaal, then races down the stairs, calling, "Ammi! Come and see!"

Finally we get to the last room. "This is our room, little buddy."

Jalaal's room—my new room—looks like a bedroom from an American show we get on Dish. From the posters that cover the wall near one of the beds, anyone can see Jalaal likes some group called the Nationals. These Nationals must be a sports team—men in uniforms throw a white ball and hit it with a round bat—but it is a sport I have never seen.

Jalaal's trophies stand at attention along two bookcase shelves, with two empty shelves below. Next to each bed is a nightstand topped with a lamp.

Jalaal points at the empty wall above my bed. "You can put up any posters you want."

I do not tell Jalaal I couldn't bring my posters. My mother said posters don't do well in suitcases, so my all-time favorite cricket stars—Omar Khan, Waqas Akram, and Arham Afridi—are still hanging on my wall back home. I look at Jalaal's sports wall and ask, "Does America have any cricket teams?"

Jalaal shakes his head. "Not any professional teams. There're a few local teams. Just adults, though." He shrugs and picks up a ball from his dresser. "Baseball is America's version of cricket. Sort of."

So that is what it's called—*baseball.*

Jalaal tosses the ball a little to my left, and I reach out and snatch it.

"Not bad, little buddy."

There is that phrase again, so I have to ask: "What does *buddy* mean?"

Jalaal smiles. "It means 'friend.'"

I am glad Jalaal thinks of me as his friend, although I am not little. Compared to Jalaal, I guess I am. But I was one of the tallest players on my cricket team this year.

I smile back at Jalaal and say, "I will call you 'big buddy.'"

He laughs, so I think he likes his new nickname.

I pass this baseball from one hand to the other. It's about the same size as a cricket ball, but not as heavy. Instead of two straight lines of stitches around the center, this one has two wavy lines, one like a frown and one like a smile. I look back at the white, round pillows on the beds and realize they are made to look like baseballs.

Jalaal holds up his hands, palms out, the universal sign for "Throw me the ball." So I do.

He catches it easily, almost like an afterthought. Plunging a hand into the pile of clothes on his bed, he fishes out a folded piece of padded leather. "Come on—let's go out back."

When we get to the bottom of the stairs, Auntie calls out, "I hope you're hungry!"

My mother turns as Jalaal and I walk past the kitchen. "Wait until you taste the *iftar* feast Auntie has prepared, Bilal! She even has a special birthday surprise for you."

I smell masala and am relieved that we are having something normal. I have heard Americans eat hot dogs, but I do not want to try those. We don't eat dog meat in Pakistan.

Jalaal opens the back door, and we step out onto a wooden terrace to the sound of some kind of motor. A man next door pushes the handle of a grass-cutting machine—Jalaal calls it a *lawn mower*. The motor is so loud that Jalaal has to yell: "This way!"

Three steps down from the terrace and we're standing on a carpet of green grass—not a single patch of dirt or sand. The grass-cutting motor fades as the man pushes the machine from the back of his house to the front.

"Here, put this on." Jalaal opens the padded leather pouch, and I stare at it.

"What is it?"

Jalaal grins. "A glove. All baseball players wear them out on the field. And the catcher, of course."

"*The* catcher? There is only one?"

"Yup."

I frown. In cricket, many players are allowed to catch the ball, not just one.

"Why do the baseball players on the field all wear gloves if only one of them can be the catcher?"

Jalaal tilts his head. "That's actually a great question."

I can tell it is not a great question.

Jalaal clears his throat. "The catcher is the one who stands behind the batter—kind of like the wicketkeeper in cricket. Any player on the field can catch the ball; they're just not called *catchers*."

"Oh. I understand."

But I don't really. It doesn't make sense—if many players are allowed to catch the ball, then why is only one called *catcher*?

Jalaal slips his left hand into his glove and punches it a few times with his right fist. "You don't wear a glove for batting, like you do in cricket. It's only for catching the ball." He takes off his glove and holds it out. "Try it."

As soon as I slip my right hand into the glove, Jalaal shakes his head. "No, no—the other hand, like this." He pulls off the glove, slides it onto my left hand, and puts the ball into my right. "There. Like that."

I wiggle my fingers, lost in the huge glove. "Actually . . . ," I start. I pull off the glove. "I need to throw with my other hand."

"Oh—you're a lefty!"

He says this in English, and I am pleased I know the words. I haven't heard of *lefty*, but I know *left* and can figure out what he meant.

"Hold on—I think there's another glove in the garage."

Jalaal trots off and comes right back with another glove. "This is my buddy's glove—he's a lefty, too."

When I put the lefty glove on my right hand, it still feels funny. All the fingers on the glove are stitched together, so I can't spread them apart. And the space for fingers is twice as long as my own fingers. Jalaal's other buddy must be a really big one.

Jalaal jogs over to a spot by the fence and punches his hand into his glove. "Ready! Go ahead—pitch me the ball."

I look at the soft grass. How is the ball supposed to bounce on grass? Maybe baseballs are specially made for grass bouncing. As a fast bowler in cricket, I'll need more room for my run-up. I back all the way to the other side of the fence.

It is hard to know how to hold this ball with these crazy, wavy stitches. I place two fingers on the top and my thumb at the bottom, and then I take off across the yard.

Jalaal's eyes widen as I race toward him. Most kids look this way when I bowl in cricket because they all know I am fast. When I get about halfway across the yard, I wind my arm and throw the ball downward, like I always do. This is when I find out baseballs do not bounce. The ball thuds and rolls toward Jalaal, coming to a pitiful stop at his feet.

Jalaal scoops it up. "I forgot to tell you that a baseball pitch is different from a cricket pitch. There's no run-up, and it's not supposed to bounce."

My shoulders slump, but I try to smile even though this baseball game is not easy to understand.

"Let's just toss the ball back and forth. We can work on pitching later."

Squinting into the fat, orange sun, I step to the right so

the big tree behind Jalaal blocks some of the light. "Okay. I am ready."

Jalaal throws the ball overhand like I did, but instead of throwing toward the ground, he launches it to my left.

I know I can catch it.

But when I step to the left out of the tree's shade, the white ball is swallowed by sunlight. I hold my glove out to where I think the ball must be. I feel the ball before I see it: a weight that slaps the fingertips of my glove, skips over the top, and lands smack on my face. On my left eye, to be exact.

Three

I sit down hard.

"Bilal! Are you okay?"

Jalaal's voice is getting closer, but I can't see him because I am holding my eye, with the other one squeezed shut. I do not cry, but maybe that is because I am ten now, not nine. Or maybe it is because I am too stunned. Or maybe when a base-ball hits you in the eye, your tears stop working.

I feel Jalaal's arms lift me from behind, and I am standing again, eyes still shut.

"Can you open that eye?"

The very last thing I want to do in this moment is open my left eye. So I open my right to find Jalaal leaning over, hands propped on his knees, peering into my good eye. He scrunches up his eyebrows.

"And the other one?" He winces. "Can you open it?"

My eye swells, a tender bump already poking into my cupped palm. I slowly remove my hand. Jalaal shakes his head.

"What?" I say, trying to sound brave. "Is it bad?"

Jalaal draws in a deep breath, then puffs his cheeks as he lets the air out. He narrows his eyes and stands up straight, hands on his waist. "I think it just needs some ice. You'll be fine."

I don't feel like I am going to be fine at all. My eye throbs, and the bump is getting even bigger, like I am growing a second head.

I follow Jalaal back inside. When we reach the kitchen, my mother gasps. "Bilal!" She rushes over, holding Humza on one hip, and takes my chin in her hand. "What happened?"

"Lal?" Humza reaches for my face, but Ammi tucks his arm back at his side.

"I was trying to catch the ball, and—"

"It was my fault," Jalaal cuts in. "A bad throw." Cold air wafts from the open freezer as Jalaal dumps a handful of ice into a plastic bag.

"Jalaal!" Auntie takes my hand and makes a clucking sound. "The poor child must be exhausted from his trip. He's in no condition to be playing baseball!"

I realize Hira has also come into the kitchen when I hear her shriek. This does not make me feel any better. She comes up and stands on her toes to inspect my eye. "Does it hurt?"

"Of course it hurts," my mother answers.

Hira leans in. "Can I touch it?"

"Touch what?" Now my uncle joins the crowd gaping at my eye. He whistles, long and low. "What happened, Bilal?"

Jalaal and I both say, "It was my fault," at exactly the same time, just as Auntie says, "It was Jalaal's doing."

I feel sorry for Jalaal and want to give him a look that says I don't blame him. But by this time my mother is pressing the ice pack onto my eye, and I have to squeeze my good eye shut so I won't cry out like a baby.

"Hold that there, Bilal," my mother says.

Auntie makes a clucking sound again and glances at the clock. "Only seven thirty—another hour until sunset. Are you hungry now, Bilal?"

"No, thank you, Auntie. I can wait." Auntie must think I am fasting for Ramadan, which makes me feel grown-up. I wanted to try fasting this year, but Ammi said to wait for next year.

I don't think I could eat anything now, anyway; my stomach feels like it is bobbing on the Arabian Sea. I look at the clock with my good eye and try to figure out what time it is back home. How can it be seven thirty in the evening when the sun is still in the sky? I hold the ice pack on my eye.

Ammi explains daylight saving time, which stretches the daylight an extra hour in the evenings. I wonder how American Muslims can wait so long to break their fast.

When the sun finally sinks behind the fence, we sit around the kitchen table. After we thank Allah and Auntie for the food, I dig into the *biryani* first. My mother makes an *mmm* sound with the first bite. "What a pleasure to have home-cooked food after those airplane meals," she says.

Hira grins through a mouthful of chicken *jalfrezi*. "Ammi, I'm going to summer camp next week, and I will meet so many friends!"

My mother smiles. "Your auntie told me. That is very kind of your uncle and auntie to send you."

"Camp?" I ask.

19

"Muslim Girl Scout camp," Auntie explains. "In the mornings, starting on Monday."

"Auntie says a Girl Scout learns many things," Hira says. "Including English."

Since I am four years older than Hira, I know more English words than she does. Not that I would go to a camp called Girl Scout. But whenever I played cricket against the boys at the International School of Karachi, I understood most of their English words.

"Bilal," Uncle says, "don't think we've left you out! You're signed up for summer baseball camp." He smiles like this is the best news in the world.

I glance at my mother, and although she is smiling, I know she is worried, because she starts fiddling with her wedding ring.

My eye feels as big as a baseball, but I say to my uncle, "Um, thank you, Mamoo. That is very kind of you."

Uncle waves his fork in my direction. "You are a talented cricket player, Bilal—I know this from your father. I have no doubt you will make him just as proud on the baseball diamond as you do on the cricket pitch."

"*Inshallah*, Mamoo," I say. *If Allah wills it.*

But if He doesn't, that would be okay with me, too.

Jalaal nods through a bite of food, then switches to English. "You've got tons of potential, Bilal."

I am not sure what *potential* means. But if it's what you need to play baseball, then I am sure I do not have any.

I look at my mother and try to make my one good eye ask, "What about cricket?" but I think she is looking only at my bad eye, because her smile is not quite as wide as it was a minute ago.

After dinner Auntie carries out a cake blazing with ten candles and sets it in front of me. The singing starts, and Hira's voice is the loudest by far. I close my eyes. Everyone probably thinks I am deciding on a wish. But my eyes are not closed for wishing—I already have a wish. My eyes are closed so I can pretend my father is here, singing and clapping along with us.

My birthday gifts are all about baseball—I receive a bat, a ball, and a glove that Uncle says he'll exchange for a lefty glove before baseball camp starts next week. Jalaal gives me a baseball cap exactly like the one he wears—dark blue with a red *W* outlined in white. He says the *W* stands for the Washington Nationals, but the loopy *W* looks like the Arabic writing for Allah. When I ask if this team is blessed by Allah, Jalaal says, "Not since 1924, when they last won the World Series."

"*Shukriya*—thank you to all of you," I say. I know that everyone is trying to make my birthday special. But I want this day to be over. I am thinking of a polite way to say that I just want to go up to bed when a loud pop makes me jump. Humza drops the empty gift box he was playing with and cries. I scoop him up and let him pull my cap off my head. I've heard gunshots in Karachi—sometimes from bad guys, but usually for celebrations like when our neighbor, Mr. Fahd, got married. Auntie and Uncle are grinning, so maybe one of their neighbors just got married, too.

Hira races down the hall and flings open the front door. "Fireworks!" By the time we step outside, she's already running across the lawn toward the street.

"Hira!" Ammi calls, but she does not sound angry. "Wait for us!"

We all help pull chairs from the garage and set them up on

the lawn. Other neighbors do the same as they wave and call, "Happy Fourth!"

My uncle points off in the distance, where another set of fireworks explodes before shimmering back down to earth. "The local high school puts on a show each year." He waves at some neighbors sitting in chairs on their lawn. "We've got the best view right here!"

Jalaal jogs over to some teenagers who stand in the street. He motions for me to join, but I pretend not to see his invitation as I adjust my chair and sit down. I don't want to insult Jalaal, or my aunt and uncle, but it feels wrong to act happy today. I don't want to share my birthday with America; I want to share it with my family—including Baba—and Mudassar and my cricket teammates and my neighbors. I want to play cricket, not baseball. I want to laugh with my friends as we watch tourists try to balance on the camels that strut down Seaview. I want to jog down to the corner shop to buy a samosa instead of floating on a chair in a sea of American houses and lawns and driveways.

To watch Hira, you would think she's not missing home at all. She has already met a girl her age called Lizzie, and they shout and turn cartwheels after each set of fireworks lights up the inky sky. Humza is happy chasing Hira and Lizzie, falling every two or three steps in the grass and picking himself up again.

My mother pats my hand but does not look at me, and that is when I know her heart feels like mine.

Our hearts want to go home.

 # Four

My eyes open before the dawn is awake on my first morning in America. From under my sheets I listen to waking-up sounds: creaking floors, soft footfalls, calls of *"Eid Mubarak—Happy Eid!"* For a moment I forget Baba is not here with us. And then weak strains of a muezzin's call to prayer drift upstairs from the TV. The call to prayer from our mosque's minarets back in Karachi flows through the streets and floats in through the windows, filling up the room. I wonder if it is prayer time back home.

Jalaal's alarm goes off—a thunk followed by a cheering crowd. He groans, fumbles for his phone on his nightstand, and silences the roaring fans. He sits up, a smudge in the dark room. He doesn't speak at first, and I wonder if he's fallen asleep sitting up. Then he rubs his face. "You awake, little buddy?"

"Yes." I pull back the sheet and swing my legs over the side of the bed.

Uncle's voice calls softly from the other side of the door: "*Eid Mubarak!*" In he steps, still in pajamas.

"*Eid Mubarak*, Baba," Jalaal says. They hug three times, then hug me three times. Seeing Uncle's *janamaz* tucked under his arm reminds me to get my own prayer mat from my suitcase.

After doing *wudu*, washing before prayer, we carry our mats downstairs into the living room and lay them out, side by side.

Everything in America is so different from Karachi. But as we recite the *Fajr* prayers, standing, then kneeling, then touching our foreheads to our prayer mats, it feels like home. If I close my eyes, I can imagine Baba right here with us.

The rest of the morning is full of *sames* and *differents*. I sink my teeth into the *sheer khurma*, and it tastes like home. The creamy milk pudding filled with thread-thin noodles, plump raisins, crunchy pistachios, and spicy cardamom is the same. But then, instead of a five-minute walk to our neighborhood mosque filled with faces I've known ever since I can remember, we drive twenty minutes to a mosque crowded with strangers.

I thought being at the mosque would feel familiar, but it does not. Lots of people there don't look like me at all. Baba has told me there are Muslims all over the world, but I am still surprised to see people who look like they come from Africa or China or even America. A thousand happy voices fill the mosque's huge entrance with greetings and laughter, and there is lots of hugging, just like home. Many people are speaking in Urdu, and I overhear some English and Arabic, too. But a few conversations are in languages I have never heard.

Some ladies are dressed like Ammi and Auntie in colorful *shalwar kameez* trousers and long shirts, their heads loosely covered with sparkly *dupatta* scarves. Others wear long dresses

24

with tighter headscarves that hide all their hair. A few ladies are so covered up that only their eyes show through narrow openings in black cloth. We break off to go to separate prayer rooms—me with Uncle and Jalaal; Ammi and Auntie with Hira and Humza.

After prayers, we go from house to house—each filled with friends of Uncle and Auntie, but they are all strangers to me. At each stop there's more *sheer khurma*—always the same. But nothing is the same.

The part of this day I look forward to most is something that has never been a part of a single Eid celebration—Skyping with my father.

◆ ◆ ◆

We gather on the living-room carpet at a low table, the computer in the middle where Humza and his sippy cup of juice can't reach the keyboard. Uncle taps some keys, and the computer makes a *boop-BEE-boop* sound. Most of the screen is black, except for a tiny window in the corner showing our faces crowded together in front of the computer. When Hira sees herself, she grins and leans closer, propping her elbows on the table and crowding me out.

"Give your brother some room," Ammi says.

Usually that would be all the invitation I'd need to elbow my way back in, but I don't want Baba to see my black eye. Ammi says she doesn't want him to worry about us. When Baba sees my eye, he'll worry.

Hira frowns and sits back on the carpet with the rest of us. Humza doesn't even pay attention to the computer until he

25

hears: "*Asalaam waalaikum*—Hello!" My father's voice sounds like he's right here with us, but we still cannot see his face. "How beautiful you all look!" I can hear the smile in his voice, but I want to see it for myself. Humza must want to see Baba's face, too, because he tries to crawl on top of the table toward the computer.

"*Bhai jaan*, my brother!" Uncle smiles and points to a small icon on our screen, even though I know Baba can't see it from our side. "Click on the camera—yours has a red line through it."

A few seconds pass before Baba says, "Ah! It is here. Can you see me now?" The black on the screen fades, replaced by my father's face. He looks confused, like he's peering into a deep, endless hole.

We cheer, and that answers Baba's question.

"I do not know how long the power will be on," Baba says, and it is only now that I realize the electricity here in America hasn't gone out yet. Maybe it goes out at night when nobody notices.

Uncle leans in and says, "I will leave you, then, to speak to your lovely family, *Bhai jaan*. *Eid Mubarak*. I only wish you could spend it with us."

Baba nods but does not speak. Sometimes my heart gets in the way of my words, and I think it is the same for Baba.

Uncle places his right hand over his heart. "Next year." He smiles. "We will all celebrate together, *inshallah*." He rises and slips from the room.

Baba reaches for the screen like he's touching our faces to make sure it's really us. Humza shrieks and claps his pudgy hands. Baba laughs.

My mother's eyes shine at this gift of seeing Baba's face.

"How is life in America? Tell me everything!"

Hira must have only heard the word *everything*, because she tells Baba every single last detail of our first twenty-four hours in America, from the green grass that tickles your bare feet to those furry, bushy-tailed rats—*squirrels*—that run everywhere here in Virginia.

When my mother finally gets a chance to talk, she is quick to praise Uncle and Auntie's hospitality. Hearing how well we've been fed and how comfortable our beds are, my father looks less worried. His face loses some of its lines, and his shoulders relax.

"How was the feast?" Ammi asks.

"We missed you." Baba's smile is sad.

It is strange to think that Baba, Daddo, and everyone in Pakistan have already celebrated the end of Ramadan, when our celebration is just starting.

Behind Baba, Daddo pads into the room, wearing her nightdress and carrying a glass of water. Her face breaks into a smile when she sees us.

"Daddo!" Hira cries, waving both hands.

My grandmother leans toward the screen, close enough that I can see the threads of silver woven through her black braid. She sighs. "I made entirely too much *jalebi* for the feast this year."

Mentioning my favorite dessert is Daddo's way of saying that she misses me, so I say, "We miss you, too, Daddo."

She blows us more kisses and then says, "I am putting these weary bones to bed. *Eid Mubarak* to all!"

She pats Baba's shoulder. "Good night, my son." He pats Daddo's hand before she turns and heads to bed. I think of all

27

the times she told stories to me before bedtime, and I wish she were here with us now.

Hira starts talking again. Listening to her, you'd think we were on vacation, having a great time. Except I am not having a great time. I should be back in our kitchen with Baba right now, sneaking a crunchy crust of a leftover samosa when Daddo isn't looking.

"Bilal?" My father's voice calls through the computer, and I realize now that my mother, Hira, and even Humza are looking at me, waiting. For what, I'm not sure. Did Baba ask me a question? I blink.

"I'm here, Baba." I move closer to the screen. For the past two days, I have been planning out all the things I want to tell Baba, and now I cannot think of a single one.

Hira, who obviously does not share my problem, blurts out, "Guess what, Baba? We saw fireworks, and I met a new friend! Her name is Lizzie."

Baba smiles. "How lucky Lizzie is to have you as a friend."

"And I am going to start Girl Scout camp on Monday. Auntie says I'll get to do swimming and make friendship bracelets and catch butterflies!"

My mother slips her arm around Hira's shoulders. "Let's give Bilal a chance now, *baytee*." She catches my eye and I smile my thanks. Ammi understands that Baba and I need time to talk without little kids around. Holding Humza on one hip, she steers Hira from the room. My sister protests: "But I didn't get to tell him that Girl Scouts go camping!" Her voice fades into the next room, and I turn back to the screen.

Baba leans forward and squints. "Bilal, what happened to your eye?"

I hope my voice sounds light when I say, "Oh, this? It is nothing." I shrug and force a grin.

"How did you get a black eye?" I hear worry in his voice as lines reappear across his forehead.

"I was playing baseball with Jalaal. Baba, do you know about baseball?" I talk faster and faster, hoping he'll forget about my eye. "It's a little bit like cricket. Next week I start baseball camp to learn how to play."

Baba tilts his head. "I have heard of baseball, but I am afraid I don't know much about it."

"That's okay, Baba. Neither do I."

Baba smiles. "You are a fine athlete, my son. You will learn this baseball game quickly."

I nod, but I am not so sure. And I don't want to waste my Skype time with Baba talking about baseball.

When Baba opens his mouth to say something, I blurt out, "When are you coming?"

Baba's lips form a straight line. Then he sighs. "As soon as I can, Bilal. I am waiting for a visa—permission from the government."

"But why did Ammi, Hira, Humza, and I get to come when you have to wait?"

Baba doesn't speak at first, like he is trying to think of the right words. And then he says, "A friend of mine in the passport office was able to arrange your visas quickly because your mother's brother already lives in America."

"So when can you get yours?"

"There is something at work that I must finish first." Baba takes off his glasses, cleans them with his shirt, and then slips them back on. "And it may take a while."

I know the "something at work" has to do with Mudassar's father.

Baba sighs. "Things are complicated right now."

I am about to say that I am old enough to hear about complicated things when Baba leans toward the screen. "I am sorry about your birthday party, Bilal *jaan*."

I don't know if I can get any words out, so I nod for now.

"I called everyone and explained that something came up unexpectedly."

"Did you call Mudassar, too?" What I really want to ask is if Baba and Mudassar's father are friends again, and if not, why?

Baba pauses. "Bilal *jaan*, there is something that you must know. Something that I cannot fully explain. Not yet."

Baba is not talking about my birthday party anymore.

"For now, you can have no contact with Mudassar."

I stare at the screen. How can such a thing come from Baba's mouth? "What do you mean? Why, Baba?"

"It will not be forever. His father and I have some things to sort out."

I want to ask how long I have to wait to talk to Mudassar—a few days? A week? But I can tell from Baba's tone that this subject is closed.

Instead, I say, "I think I am already forgetting."

"Forgetting?"

My shoulders slump. "About home. I mean, I remember what everything looks like. But we only just left, and already I am forgetting what home sounds like, what it smells like."

Baba seems to consider my question. Then his eyes smile. "Today smelled like rain. Loud rain—too much rain! Our first proper monsoon of the season."

"Did Mrs. Ahmed get her laundry in time?"

Baba nods. "Luckily for my ears, today she remembered."

I grin. No one ever sees Mrs. Ahmed's laundry because she puts it out to dry on her balcony directly below ours. But when she forgets to bring it in during monsoon season and the rain soaks it through, even Mr. Ali can hear her shouting nine floors below when he reopens his tea cart after the rain.

My grin fades. "What if I forget everything?"

"You won't, Bilal *jaan*."

For the second time in my life, I don't know if I believe my father.

Then I have an idea. "Stay right here, Baba."

He laughs. "Where else would I go?"

I race from the room, grab the pad of paper and pencil near the kitchen phone, and then dart back to the computer screen.

I jot something down on the pad and then hold it up.

Baba leans in, adjusts his glasses, and reads my writing:

- The smell of rain during monsoon season
- Mrs. Ahmed's laundry-screeching voice

I place the pencil and paper on the table, next to the keyboard. "When we talk or write, I will trade you one new thing in America for one Karachi memory. That way, you will know what to expect when you get here, and I will remember everything about Karachi."

"I like that idea." Baba nods, and holds up a hand. "Stay right here."

I laugh. "Where else would I go?"

Baba disappears for a few seconds, and then he's back in

front of the screen, holding up a notebook and a pen. "I've given you one memory—no, two! Now it is your turn."

How to begin? Everything is new here—I could list a million things. "You told me today smelled like rain. In America, it smells like cut grass. Gardens here have grass carpets called *lawns*, and people like to cut the grass with a machine. And if the cut grass gets on the sidewalk, they blow it away with another machine."

Baba shakes his head like he can't believe such a thing. He writes on his paper, then holds it up for me to see:

• The scent of cut grass

"I have started my list," Baba declares. "When I miss you, which is a hundred times a day, I will look at the list and it will feel like I am right there with you."

I hold up my thumb to the computer's camera for Baba to see. "In America, a thumb sticking up means something is good. Jalaal told me." I raise my other thumb and grin. "Your idea is a two-thumbs-up idea."

I wait to see how Baba reacts, because a thumb up in Pakistan is definitely not the kind of gesture for good ideas. In fact, Mudassar got sent home from school one time when he did this to Yusef, who said Mudassar's sister smelled like a camel.

Baba's eyes grow wide, and then he laughs louder and longer than I have heard him laugh for many months. I laugh, too, and soon we are both wiping away tears and catching our breath.

"I don't recommend you share this new custom with Daddo. Your grandmother would not appreciate the humor like we do." Baba picks up his pen. "But I have heard of this American gesture. I am going to write that down."

My mother's voice calls from the kitchen. "Bilal, time to let your father go to sleep. It is the middle of the night back home."

I sigh.

Baba laughs. "Tell your mother I heard that. And she is right. We will talk again tomorrow."

"Okay. Good night, Baba."

"Take care of that eye."

"I will."

He blows me a kiss, and I catch it and press it on my heart. I blow him one back, and he does the same.

My hand hovers over the touch pad before I guide the cursor to the icon of the red phone, but I don't want to click it.

Baba must feel the same way, because he says, "On three, okay?"

I nod.

"One, two . . . three."

I still don't click on the red phone, but Baba does, because there's a *booping* sound, and then he's gone.

The clanking of pots and spoons drifts in from the kitchen, mixed with Ammi and Auntie's laughter. Usually the feast is my favorite part of Eid, even though we have to dress up. There will be gifts of money for my sister and brother, my cousin, and me. We'll drink *lassi*, made of sweet yogurt, and eat until our stomachs won't hold another bite. Then we'll have dessert.

But today I have already had my favorite part of Eid— Skyping with Baba.

Five

As soon as I walk into the gym with Jalaal, anyone can see I'm different from the other kids at baseball camp. I'm the only one with a black eye.

Kids stand in clumps around signs with words I have never seen before, like Dylan's Dugout Crew and Hank's Home Run Champs. I swallow.

Jalaal scans the gym. "Your group is here somewhere." He takes off his cap. I take mine off, too. I look around but have no idea which group is mine. Jalaal is one of the high school camp trainers, but not for my group. I wish he could be my camp trainer in case I have any questions. Maybe someone in my group will speak Urdu. If not, I will try my best in English, but I don't know very many baseball words. Thanks to Jalaal, I do know *glove*, *catcher*, and *pitch*, and that is better than nothing.

"There's your coach," Jalaal says, flipping his cap back onto his head. "I'll introduce you."

I flip my own cap back on and follow Jalaal over to a sign with more new words: Matt's Mad Dog Mavericks. I smile, because even though I don't know all these words, I do know what a mad dog is. Then I stop smiling, because what do mad dogs have to do with baseball? Maybe the mad dog is our mascot. But dogs are dirty creatures that run in the streets. Who would want a dog for a mascot?

Jalaal calls, "Hey!" to a man with short hair the color of strong tea. They do a very complicated handshake, ending with a sort of hug and a fist-thump on each other's back. I hope the coach doesn't greet me that way, because I'll never remember the hand motions. Luckily, he just sticks out his hand and says, "I'm Coach Matt. How're you doing, big guy?"

This is the second nickname someone has given me here in America. I wonder if I'm supposed to give people nicknames, too.

I shift my baseball bag to my other shoulder and shake Coach Matt's hand. "Hello, sir. My name is Bilal."

Coach Matt smiles. I can tell he is older than Jalaal, because he really needs to shave. Or maybe he is trying to grow a beard. But he isn't old like my parents. He turns his baseball cap around backward. "Welcome to camp, Bilal."

"Thank you, sir."

He gives my shoulder a side punch, and I take a small step sideways. Not because it was a hard punch, but because I wasn't expecting it.

"You can call me Coach Matt."

"Okay, Coach Matt, sir."

Jalaal bends down and whispers in Urdu, "He means you can drop the 'sir.' Just 'Coach Matt,' or 'Coach,' is fine."

35

I feel my ears go hot. It's one thing to know words in English, but another thing to know which words to use when and which words to leave out.

Jalaal pats my shoulder and announces, "Well, I'm off." He nods toward the opposite side of the gym before walking away. "See you later, little buddy," he calls over his shoulder.

"Good-bye, big buddy."

I want to run after him, but I know I can't. Instead I take a breath and turn to join my group.

The Matt's Mad Dog Mavericks sign is surrounded by boys my age, all except for a tall boy with yellow curls sticking out from under his cap. This boy is big like Jalaal and throws his head back when he laughs at something one of the other boys says. He reaches over and punches a kid on the shoulder like Coach Matt did to me. The boy grins and punches him back. Obviously, shoulder punching is an American sign of friendship.

When Coach Matt calls, "Hey, Kyle!" the yellow-haired boy jogs over.

"This is Kyle," Coach Matt says to me. "He's one of the high school camp trainers who'll be helping us out." He turns to Kyle. "This is Bilal."

Kyle sticks out his hand and says, "Good to meet you, Bilal." He narrows his eyes. "Wow, nice shiner."

"Thank you," I say, wishing I knew what a shiner is.

Coach Matt adjusts his cap. "Bilal is Jalaal's cousin. Just got here from Pakistan."

"Right." Kyle nods. "Jalaal told us you were coming. We play together on the high school team. You play baseball in Pakistan?"

"No, it is my first time."

I don't tell Kyle this is actually my second time; Black-Eye Day doesn't count.

"Okay, Mad Dogs!" Coach Matt claps his hands and rubs them together. "Have a seat, gentlemen!"

But when I look around, there are no seats. Tennis shoes squeak on shiny wood as the boys gather closer and sit on the floor. I sit, too.

"First of all, Mad Dogs, welcome to baseball camp!" Coach Matt sounds very excited about this day. The other boys clap and yell things like "Yeah!" and "Woo!" and pump their fists in the air. I pretend to be happy, too. I even yell, "Yeah!" like the others, but secretly I am praying I will get through the day without another black eye.

Coach Matt continues. "I remember most of you from last year's camp and the regular season. We've got a few new faces this time, so let's go around and introduce ourselves. Give us your name and the position you like to play best."

I stare at Coach Matt. He talks too fast for me to understand all of his words. He points to one boy and asks him to stand.

"Jake, second base."

The next boy stands and says, "Akash, catcher."

They are saying their names. That much I know. And of course I know *catcher* is a position in baseball. One I will never play.

The boys continue to stand, one by one:

"Carlos, second base."

"Jack, shortstop."

"Aiden, left field."

And it goes on this way until it is my turn.

"Bilal," I say, and now I need to pick a position.

In cricket I play the gully position most, but I didn't hear anyone say this one, so I don't think it is a baseball word. I try to think of what the boy next to me just said.

"Um, third base?" I sit down quickly and hope third base is something like the gully position.

"Great!" Coach Matt nods. "Okay, Mad Dogs, here's how we'll run the day."

I figured there would be running, which I don't mind. But as Coach Matt talks and talks, I only understand a few of his words. How can this be? I can speak English. But Coach Matt's American English does not sound the same as the English I learned from Madam Sughra last year. The other kids laugh at some things Coach Matt says. I laugh along, too, so no one will suspect that I do not understand the jokes.

All at once the boys scramble to their feet and head outside with their bags slung over their shoulders. I am the last to follow.

We skirt around an asphalt-covered area where other kids are gathered, listening to a coach who is the tallest man I have ever seen. Coach Matt leads us up some concrete steps with dry grass poking through cracks. It is hard to grow grass in Karachi, but here grass grows all over the place.

At the top of the steps is a field so green it hurts my eyes. I watch the other kids so I'll know what to do. They dig into their bags and pull out their gloves before flinging their bags onto the bottom bench of the shiny metal bleachers. I do the same, then jog out to where Coach Matt and Kyle are waiting.

After showing us some throws, the coaches pair us up for practice.

Coach Matt waves a kid over. "Akash, this is Bilal. He's from Pakistan. Isn't that where you're from?"

38

Akash shakes his head. "I'm from here." He shrugs. "My parents are from India."

"Close enough, right?" Coach Matt says. He pats Akash on the shoulder and walks away to pair up more kids.

India and Pakistan are close—they are right next to each other—but for some reason Akash does not look happy about Coach Matt's words.

I pull on my glove. "You move here from India?"

Akash shakes his head. "Never been."

I stare at him. "Never?"

He stares back, like a challenge. "Nope." And he goes back to tossing the ball and catching it in his glove.

I want to ask him what it's like to be from a different country than his parents, but I do not know him well enough to ask such a question. Plus he doesn't look like he wants to talk. Maybe if we become the kind of friends who punch each other's shoulders and call each other by nicknames, then I will ask him this question.

Akash backs up a few steps. "Ready?" He holds up the ball like the point of a question mark, and I nod even though I am not ready, even though I will never be ready. I glance around to be sure no one is behind me if—*when*—I miss the ball.

I give my glove a few punches with my left fist like I've seen the other boys do.

Akash pulls his arm back and lifts one knee. He lets the ball fly, and I jump for it. The ball hits my glove near the thumb, then skips over the edge and drops behind me. I scoop up the ball. When I turn back, I think I see Akash rolling his eyes.

Looking around at the others, I can tell I am the worst player out here. I must have been terrible at cricket when I first

39

learned, but that was too many years ago to remember. Back then I wasn't the only one learning to play, so we were all bad at cricket together. But when I think about it, even Omar Khan, the greatest cricket player in the history of the world, wasn't born knowing how to play cricket. He had to start somewhere, and I guess now I do, too. With baseball.

Akash punches his glove, waiting for me to throw the ball. I know now that I am supposed to pitch the ball, not bowl it as I did in cricket. Eyeing Akash's glove, I pull back my arm and take a step as I let the ball fly. Akash barely has to move, because the ball finds its way right where I told it to go—into the soft leather center of his glove.

Akash stands up straight and pushes his hat back. "Man! Nice one, Bilal."

The compliment fills my chest. "Thank you."

Now it's his turn to throw, but as soon as Akash lets the ball go, I have an idea—a lightning-quick thought. I whip off my glove and let it drop to the ground as I reach up, a little to the left, and snatch the ball out of the air.

Akash shakes his head and grins. "I cannot believe you caught that."

I smile even though my hand stings.

He points at the glove lying at my feet. "You're not gonna use that?"

I shake my head. "I catch better without it."

"You play baseball in Pakistan?" Akash asks.

I lift the brim of my cap a centimeter. "No—cricket."

Akash nods. "My dad's played before."

A spark of hope flickers in my chest. "Here in America?"

"Nah. Back in India."

The spark snuffs itself out.

We toss the ball back and forth some more until Coach Matt yells, "Okay, Mad Dogs! Now that you're warmed up, let's try a throw-off. We're going to get some baseline info so we can track your progress from now through the end of camp."

Akash must see confusion on my face, because he jogs over and explains what *throw-off* means. I don't understand all of his words—he talks fast like Coach Matt—but I understand when Akash points to two targets hanging from a fence.

"You'll be good at this," Akash says.

"I don't know." I try to sound like it doesn't matter. But it will matter if I make a fool of myself in front of everyone.

We form two lines across from the two targets.

"Okay, Mad Dogs! Remember what I said about sports-manship."

I have no idea what *sportsmanship* means, never mind what he said about it.

"We're here to support each other—boost each other's spirits. We're here to have fun, and to learn to play ball. Let me hear you now, Mad Dogs—we're here to have fun and to . . ."

"Play ball!" everyone shouts. Everyone except me, because I did not know I was supposed to yell these words.

The first boy in each line stands behind a rope, and when Coach Matt blows a whistle, they each launch a baseball at the target. One ball misses, and the other smacks the top.

Coach Matt writes something on a clipboard. "Nice effort, Andy and Carter! Next up!"

The boy whose ball hit the target jogs to the end of his line, but the boy who missed goes off to the side to watch.

Two other boys step up to the rope, and Coach Matt blows

his whistle again. As more players take their turns, I figure out that whoever hits the target goes back in line for another turn. Those who miss gather on the side to yell good things to the boys who are still in.

My turn comes up, and I hit the target easily, just to the right of the center. When all of us have had a turn, Coach Matt and Kyle move the rope back about a meter, so now we're farther away from the targets.

I make it through the next round, and the round after that, until the rope puts us twice as far from the target as when we started. Only two of us are left. Akash yells, "That's it, Bilal! You got this!"

The rest of the boys clap and hoot, some yell my name, and others yell the name Jordan. I close my eyes for a few seconds, and it's like I'm back home on the cricket pitch. I breathe, open my eyes, and turn my attention to the target.

Coach Matt's whistle pierces the air. I draw my arm back and then let the baseball fly. Jordan's baseball thwacks the center of the target a split second before my ball lands—too far to the right.

The boys erupt into cheers.

I decide second place is okay. For now.

I turn to congratulate Jordan, but he is already surrounded by some of the other kids.

"Nice, Bilal!" Akash calls, and the others head toward me, their hands ready for high fives. It is when they leave Jordan behind to congratulate me that I realize Jordan is not a "he" at all.

Jordan is a girl.

 Six

We've only been home from camp twenty minutes when I find Jalaal out on the porch, slumped on the front step like a half-empty sack of rice. He passes a baseball from one hand to the other, elbows propped on his knees. He's not watching the ball, though; he is staring at the driveway of the house next door, like he's hoping it will notice him.

"*Salaam*, Jalaal," I say, and sit down. He looks like he could use a buddy.

"Hey, Bilal." His eyes don't leave the driveway, and his hands don't stop passing that ball back and forth, back and forth.

"Do you want to play catch?" This is brave of me to offer, considering. But it might make Jalaal feel better, and maybe it would help me forget about losing to a girl today.

"Nah." He shrugs. "Too hot."

Jalaal hands me the ball, and I continue his back-and-forth ritual. It is kind of relaxing. "What are you doing out here?"

Jalaal sighs. "Just hanging."

He says this in English, and although it doesn't look like he's hanging on to anything, I nod anyway. Sometimes men don't need to explain everything. It makes me think of Baba and my uncles, who can sit outside the tea shop down the street and not say anything for ten minutes—they just sip and look out at the sea.

Jalaal finally looks at me. "So what'd you think of your first day of camp?"

I'm not sure how to answer. Jalaal loves baseball, and I can tell he wants me to love it, too. I decide to answer his question with a question. "Do girls play baseball?"

At first he looks confused, then he nods. "Right, that girl— what's her name again? Jen? Jessie?"

"Jordan. Like the country."

He snaps his fingers. "That's it—Jordan. She's Coach Matt's niece. She and her mom just moved here—from Illinois, I think. Or maybe Iowa."

I've never heard of either of those cities.

Jalaal shrugs. "She'll probably join a softball team in the fall, but it was too late to sign up for a summer camp. Coach said he'd let her play."

I've never heard of softball. If the ball is soft, it must not be a batting game.

Before I can ask Jalaal anything else about Jordan, the yellow car with the white flower hubcaps pulls into the driveway next door.

Jalaal pops up to his feet so fast he startles me, and I drop the ball. But he doesn't even notice because he's already halfway across the lawn, jogging toward the neighbor's driveway.

A girl steps out of the car, and her hair is as orange as a *kinnoo* fruit. I've seen pictures of people with this kind of hair, but now that I see it in real life, I cannot stop staring. Her hair is curly and falls down her back. The minute she turns and sees Jalaal, her whole face breaks into a smile.

Jalaal isn't even acting like himself. Not that I have known him very long, but the way he is standing, with his arms folded, anyone can see he is nervous. But a happy nervous, with a lopsided grin. I run to catch up.

"Bilal, this is Olivia. Olivia—my cousin Bilal." Jalaal's cheeks look flushed. It makes me want to hand him a glass of water.

"It is nice to meet you, Olivia."

She smiles a Bollywood movie-star smile with those straight, white teeth, and I notice tiny brown spots sprinkled across her nose and cheeks.

She holds her hand out. "Welcome to America, Bilal."

I've never shaken a girl's hand before. When I look at Jalaal, he nods in her direction, so I reach out my hand. She has a strong handshake. Her khaki shorts have smudges of dirt, and her dark green T-shirt says "The Other Side Nursery: Where the grass is always greener!" I don't stare at her dirty clothes, because maybe she feels embarrassed. Olivia pulls her hair back, twists it up, then takes a brown plastic clip from the end of her sleeve and sticks it in her hair. With all that hair up and away from her face, her skin reminds me of a marble statue—pale and smooth. Except for those tiny flecks of brown.

Jalaal stands there, transfixed, but Olivia doesn't seem to notice. "It's way too humid today. I must look like a lion." She smooths a stray curl behind her ear, but it springs back into place.

Jalaal laughs and shakes his head. "You look great."

Olivia smiles and punches him in the shoulder. I know this means they're friends, but even I can tell they aren't the kind of friends like Jalaal and Kyle, or like me and Mudassar back home.

"Jalaal!" Auntie's voice carries across the lawn from our driveway, where she stands beside the minivan.

"Coming!" he calls over his shoulder, and his smile slides right off his face.

Olivia looks at me and says, "It was nice to meet you, Bilal. I'll see you around."

"Good-bye, Olivia." I wave, then race to the driveway where Auntie waits, holding a bag of groceries. Her eyes narrow as she watches Jalaal stride across the grass toward us. All the light has gone out of his face.

Auntie hands Jalaal a bag, her eyes on his the whole time. He spins around with the groceries and heads inside.

"I can take some, Auntie."

She touches my cheek, finally looking away from Jalaal. "Thank you, Bilal, but I can get these last two bags." She nods toward the open door of the minivan. "Why don't you wake your sister and bring her in out of this heat."

I peek into the van to find Hira fast asleep, her head back and her mouth open. In one hand she clutches a paper bag. Around her wrist is a bracelet woven from colorful threads. I tap her arm gently and her eyes fly open.

"Are we home?"

She tries to push herself off the seat before remembering she is still wearing her seat belt. I unbuckle it for her and she reaches into the bag.

"Look what I made at camp!"

She pulls out a bookmark made from yellow flowers pressed between two strips of clear plastic. Some of the petals are wrinkled and one is torn, but I can tell she worked hard on it.

"Nice, Hira."

She takes my hand and leaps from the van. "It's for you!" She thrusts the bookmark at me. "The flowers are called *buttercups*." This last word she says in English, and we laugh that a flower is named after butter.

"Are you sure you wouldn't rather give this to Ammi or Auntie?"

Hira seems to consider this. "I can make more tomorrow. This one is for you."

"Thank you, Hira." I smile, but silently vow never to be seen with a buttercup bookmark outside this house.

As we head up the driveway, Hira asks, "What did you make at baseball camp?"

I shake my head. "You don't make anything at baseball camp—you *play* baseball."

"Oh." Hira frowns. "Was it fun?"

I think about coming in second place in the throwing contest, which was fun up until the part where I found out that a girl beat me. I shrug. "Some of it was fun, I guess."

We get to the shade of the porch, and Hira heads straight for the swing. She settles herself onto the bench seat and holds up her wrist. "This is a friendship bracelet. I can teach you how to make one—it's easy."

Hira's feet can't quite reach the floor, so I push the swing with the toe of my sneaker while she describes in detail how to make a friendship bracelet. She says some of the words in English, like *thread* and *weave*.

I give the swing another push. "Did you understand every-thing at camp today?"

Hira looks up from her bracelet and shakes her head. "But I watched. And one girl speaks Urdu, so she helped me."

I wish someone at baseball camp spoke Urdu besides Jalaal, who doesn't even work with my group.

Ammi opens the front door and pokes her head out. "I want to hear all about your day." She smiles. "Your auntie just finished making cookies with chocolate bits. They are delicious. Tidy up your rooms and then it will be time for tea."

Hira frowns. "Ammi, do I have to clean my room now? Can't I do it later?"

Ammi kneels in front of Hira and pats her knee. "*Baytee*, this is not our home. We must always be respectful and show our thanks to Uncle and Auntie. They are very kind to take us in until Baba can get here and we can look for a home of our own."

But we already have a home back in Karachi. I don't say this, because even though Ammi wears a smile, her eyes are shiny. My heart feels like it's stuck in my throat.

"Come on, Hira." We stand, and the swing knocks into the back of my legs.

Ammi takes Hira's hand. "Besides, the sooner you clean your rooms, the sooner you will get to taste Auntie's cookies."

After a month of the adults fasting until sundown, it sounds strange to hear Ammi talk about eating in the middle of the day.

When I get to my room—Jalaal's and my room—it is a mess. Clothes have been tossed on both beds and the floor. One clean-looking stack of folded clothes sits on Jalaal's desk.

Others are definitely dirty, like Jalaal's camp uniform dumped in the middle of the carpet. None of these clothes are mine.

I start to leave but find Ammi in the hall. "Have you finished?"

"No, but—"

"I'm done!" Hira calls from her doorway.

Ammi peeks into my room. "Bilal, get going."

"They're all Jalaal's clothes, Ammi!"

She lowers her voice. "It doesn't matter, Bilal. I don't want Auntie walking by and thinking this mess is yours."

I bite my lip. I am not cleaning up Jalaal's mess.

Ammi's face softens. "Just drape his clothes on the back of his desk chair, and then come down and join us."

I step back into the room and sigh. I never had to keep my room so clean before. Now here I am in a room that's not even mine, picking up someone else's dirty socks.

I finish piling Jalaal's clothes on his chair and add the last T-shirt to the pile just as my cousin walks in.

"Hey, little buddy." He stops short. "Wow! You didn't have to pick up my stuff."

I fold my arms. "Yes, I did. Ammi said I had to."

Jalaal's face falls. "Oh, man. Sorry. I was looking for my camp T-shirt this morning and couldn't find it."

"That's okay," I say.

Jalaal grabs his car keys and heads out, calling, "Catch you later, little buddy!"

I don't want to play catch later. Just like I don't want to live in someone else's room. Of all the things I miss about Karachi, I never guessed I would miss picking up my own dirty clothes off my own bedroom floor.

Seven

After one week of baseball camp, I am still no good at hitting a ball with a bat. But I have been practicing my English and learning all kinds of new baseball words from Akash and the other kids—words like *grand slam* and *strike zone* and *home run*. I also learned new meanings for words I thought I already knew—like *safe*, *single*, *double*, *triple*, *base*, and *home*.

After camp today Akash catches up with me on my way to the parking lot.

"Man, it's a hot one today."

I have noticed Americans say *man* a lot, so I say, "Yes, man. It is hot."

"Hey, you wanna hit the pool later?"

Maybe hitting the pool means hitting the water, like a dive or a belly flop. Whatever it means, I think this is my first chance at having a real friend in America, so I say yes, I will come to the pool.

Akash comes over later with another boy from camp named Henry, and the three of us head out, towels slung over our shoulders. The whole way to the pool, all they can talk about is how Jordan beat Henry in the batting contest yesterday.

"You were just having an off day, man." Akash shrugs. "Don't worry about it."

Henry sighs. "Easy for you to say—she didn't beat you."

"You both beat me," I offer. But then again, so did everyone else.

Henry nods. "Yeah, but only because you've been playing baseball for exactly one week your whole entire life."

That makes me feel a little better.

We turn down another street that leads to a parking lot. A low, white building sits at the end. A big sign posted next to the open double doors reads, "Swim Meet Tomorrow—Go Marlins!"

Swim meet? Do swimmers go there to meet each other?

We duck out of the sun into the lifeguard office. Waves of light from the pool shimmer across the ceiling, and the smell of sun cream mingles with steaming pizza. We have to sign our names in a book. My hand hovers over the right side of the paper for a second before I remember to write my name in English letters starting on the left.

The boys' locker room smells exactly like the one at the pool I used to go to in Karachi—part soap, part cleaning solution, and part chlorine. Once we step out into the pool area, I squint in the bright sun. Akash and Henry toss their towels onto lounge chairs and head for the diving board. I drop my towel next to theirs and turn to follow, but then I stop. I blink. I cannot believe it.

51

Everyone is wearing a bathing suit. And not just kids, but fathers and mothers and grandparents, too.

Back in Karachi we went to the beach all the time, but adults always covered themselves with regular clothes—light *shalwar kameez* trousers and long shirts, no arms or legs or shoulders sticking out. At the club pool there were swimming hours for ladies and children, and swimming hours for men and children, but never together.

But here, in America? Aren't the adults embarrassed to be half-naked in front of everyone? This will definitely go on my American list of things for Baba to know. I will tell him not to share it with Daddo, because I think my grandmother would have a heart attack.

I head to the diving board, my eyes focusing on my feet slapping across the wet pavement.

It turns out we're so busy jumping and diving and flipping off the board that I almost forget about the half-naked adults. Akash and Henry teach me how to do jumps called *cannonball* and *jackknife*. I teach them how to dive headfirst, arms at our sides, until one lifeguard blows his whistle and tells us we are not allowed to do that.

We're in the middle of a new game called Marco Polo when both lifeguards stand on high platforms and blow their whistles at the same time—high, then low, then high.

Akash groans. "Already?"

"Come on, Bilal." Henry pulls himself out of the water. "It's break."

Why do we have to take a break? I climb up the ladder, wiping the water from my eyes. From somewhere behind me near the diving board, Henry calls, "Hey, Mrs. Wu!"

I turn to see Akash waving. He doesn't seem to care that he is talking to a lady in a bathing suit.

"Fancy meeting you boys here—again." The lady laughs as she squeezes water from her ponytail and adjusts her white plastic sunglasses. "How is baseball camp going?"

"Pretty good," Henry says, then turns to me. "This is Bilal—he just moved here."

"Bilal, did you say?" She holds her hand out.

I cannot believe I am shaking hands with a lady wearing a bathing suit. "Hello, Madam." But I don't meet her eyes—I can't. Instead, I stare at her bright yellow flip-flops. Her toenails are painted sky blue, with a white cloud on each big toe.

Akash shakes his head like he has water in his ear. "Do you know if we're in your class next year?"

Mrs. Wu shakes her head. "We won't get our class lists until next month, in August." She waves to someone across the pool. "Enjoy your afternoon, boys." And then she's off.

Class lists?

"Mrs. Wu's one of the best teachers in the school," Henry says. "My sister had her two years ago. I hope we're all in her class this year."

We sit at the side of the pool, our legs dangling in the water, as the guys fill me in on the rest of the fifth-grade teachers. I can't remember all of their names, but I do remember that I don't want to get Mr. Fike, who makes kids do unfinished homework during recess.

As we head back to our chairs, Henry mutters, "Oh, great."

I follow his gaze past the fence to the bike racks, where Jordan frees her curly ponytail from underneath her helmet.

She spots us and waves.

53

The others turn and pretend not to see her. I wave back and she smiles.

"Bilal!" Henry whisper-yells. "Now she's gonna come over."

Jordan disappears into the lifeguard office, and Henry acts fast, spreading our towels out on three chairs. A fourth chair is still open. "Quick—hand me your goggles," he says to Akash. With the goggles sitting in the middle of the last chair, it looks like all four lounge chairs are taken.

Jordan emerges from the locker room with a towel over one shoulder and sunglasses perched on top of her head.

Henry sighs. "I can't believe this."

"Let it go, man," Akash says under his breath. "There's no room for her over here—she'll have to find somewhere else to put her stuff."

"Hi, guys," Jordan says.

"Hey," they mumble, looking toward the pool, back at the snack bar, anywhere but at the girl standing in front of them.

"Hi, Jordan," I say.

Her smile fades as she glances at the other guys.

The lifeguards' whistle signals the end of break, followed by the sound of a hundred splashes as kids jump back into the pool.

Jordan unties one tennis shoe and slips it off, hopping on one foot, then does the same with the other. "Are these your chairs?" she asks, her shoes now dangling from her fingers.

Akash and Henry look at each other. "Um, yeah, they are." Henry crosses his arms.

"Great." Jordan tucks her shoes under a chair.

Henry swipes his towel from the same chair. "Look, guys, I got to get going."

Akash slides his feet into his shoes and grabs his towel. "Me, too."

Jordan looks at the clock. "It's only five. You guys have to leave already?"

Akash nods. "See you around at camp."

They walk away, but my feet aren't ready to move yet. Jordan puts her hands on her hips and looks out at the water. "Are you staying?"

"Hey, Bilal," Henry calls. "Come on!"

I look at the guys waiting for me and then back at Jordan, who slides her sunglasses from the top of her head onto her face. "Looks like you gotta go. I'll see you later."

Halfway to the locker room, I turn back and see Jordan standing alone in front of four empty chairs. Part of me wants to go back, because maybe Jordan is missing a faraway friend like I am missing Mudassar. But even if she is, at least Jordan could still call her friend back home. Baba says I still can't talk to Mudassar.

"Bilal!" Akash sticks his head out from the locker room. "You coming or what?"

Turning away from Jordan, I duck into the shade of the locker room and follow Akash and Henry back outside. All the way home they joke and talk about baseball. I understand some of their words and none of their punch lines. The blazing sun begins to slip behind the tallest trees. I wish I were looking at a Karachi moon instead, talking and laughing with Mudassar.

Eight

I have to take an English test before I start school next month. If it is the kind of English I learned in Karachi, then I will do well. If it is the kind of English everyone has been using at baseball camp for the past three weeks, then I am in trouble. I thought I would learn more English here in America; instead, I have learned how much English I still don't understand.

I pause in the steamy heat outside a low, brick building where my fate will be decided. A bead of sweat rolls down the back of my neck. My only consolation is that Hira has to take this test, too. Auntie pulls the front door open and my sister skips into the building.

"Bilal?" Ammi beckons me to hurry inside. "We don't want to be late."

We? *I* would actually love to be late.

I sigh, passing under an arctic blast of air-conditioning that makes me shiver. Hira and I follow Auntie and Ammi down a hallway and into an office. Behind a tall counter I can see the top of a pair of glasses worn by a woman with hair gathered into a sleek bun. My mother fills out some forms as Humza plays with the strap of her sandal. The lady leads Hira and me to separate rooms for our tests. My sister doesn't look nervous at all. I shake my head. She has no idea how much English she still has to learn.

When I enter my testing room, I almost fall over in surprise when one lady greets me in Urdu.

"Hello! I'm Mrs. Fayad. It is nice to meet you . . ."—she glances at the papers in her hand—"Bilal."

I recover in time to say, "It is nice to meet you, too, Madam."

She smiles and looks to another woman standing beside her. "Mrs. Wilson will be administering your English test today, Bilal. I'll be translating for you as needed."

Why does she need to translate in Urdu if it's supposed to be a test of English?

Mrs. Wilson begins with easy questions, asking me where I am from and what I like to do. When I talk about cricket, she looks confused, and I hope this does not lower my score. But Mrs. Fayad smiles and nods, so maybe it will all turn out okay.

Mrs. Wilson hands me a book and tells me a little bit about the story, then asks me what I think will happen in the story.

How am I supposed to know? I glance at the picture of the boy and the dog on the book's cover. The dog does not look like he will bite the boy, but I don't know for sure—maybe the boy found the dog wandering in the street. Maybe when the boy's mother finds out he is touching the dog, she will get very mad and make the boy take an extra-long shower. Then I remember that Americans have dogs for pets. I decide this is a trick question, so to be safe, I say, "I don't know what will happen in the story."

Mrs. Wilson nods, then asks me to read the story aloud. I freeze. What if I make mistakes? How many mistakes can I make and still pass the test?

I look at the first sentence, and I don't even know how to say the first word. I read the whole first sentence in my head and realize the first word is the dog's name. I have never heard of this name, and I am not sure how to say it.

"Anytime you're ready to begin," Mrs. Wilson says, tapping the eraser side of her pencil on the paper in front of her.

I take a breath. "Har—Har—vay?" I begin, then wait for her to correct me.

"Harvey." She nods like she's agreeing with me, but the name she said was different from the way I said it.

I swallow. "Harvey was a good dog—" Then I get to another word I don't know. "Us . . . usoo . . . usoo-a-lee?"

"Usually," Mrs. Wilson says, with that same nod.

It goes like this for another few sentences, until she finally says, "You're doing a great job, Bilal, but let's try a different book."

I am not doing a great job. Mrs. Wilson never thought I was doing a great job, either, because next she gives me a baby book—a story with only one sentence on each page. I read every single word with no mistakes.

"Hmm," Mrs. Wilson says. "Let's try something in the middle."

So then I have to read another book with some hard words but not too many. Mrs. Wilson seems happy with that, and I let out a breath. Maybe now the test is over. Except it's not—

now I have to tell what happened in the story. After that Mrs. Wilson asks me if I have a connection to the story. I don't know what this means, so I say no. Then she asks me what message the author is trying to tell me. Is there a secret message in the story? If so, I have no idea what it is.

"Now on to the writing," Mrs. Wilson says. She slides a piece of lined paper and a pencil over to me and says, "Write about what you've done over the summer."

I look at that single sheet of paper and think there are not enough lines for everything I could write about this summer. I could write that when my father disappeared, it was the worst three days of my entire life. And the day he came back was the best day. I could write that I thought everything would go back to normal once Baba came back, but then it didn't; we left almost everything we owned and came to America, where I don't understand most of what people are saying, and I am learning a game called baseball that doesn't make any sense, and I miss playing cricket with my friends.

The lines swim before my eyes, and suddenly I am tired. Tired of English and tired of not feeling smart, tired of missing my father, and tired of living in a house that is not mine. Just tired.

"Bilal?" Mrs. Fayad says my name softly, then continues in Urdu: "This is for writing." She pats the paper. "Here is where you can write about what you did this summer."

"Whenever you're ready, Bilal," Mrs. Wilson says.

I nod, then write:

This summer I move to America. I learn baseball.
I miss Pakistan.

I hand her the paper. She looks surprised, but she takes it from me and scans my writing. "Do you want to add anything else?"

"No, thank you, Madam."

I stand.

Mrs. Fayad smiles and says, "Well done," but I can tell Mrs. Wilson doesn't think I did well at all. She leads me out to where my mother and Auntie are waiting. As soon as they see me, their eyes open wide in a way that means, "How did it go?" I shrug and slip into the seat next to my mother. Humza sleeps in his stroller. He is lucky to be so little. He does not have to take tests or go to school or learn more English.

Five minutes later Hira comes bounding out the door, holding a lady's hand and looking like she's won a prize.

We get the results of our tests, and now I know why Hira is so happy. "Her English is coming along beautifully," says the lady, who introduces herself in Urdu as Mrs. Hakim.

Auntie smiles at Hira. "My niece and nephew were learning English in school back in Pakistan and are good students."

Mrs. Hakim beams at my sister. "Hira is a level 3 ESL student, which means she'll likely be monitored in her regular classroom by an ESL teacher in case she needs support. She will only be pulled out of class for extra help when she needs it, not on a regular basis. She should do fine in the regular classroom setting."

Ammi smiles at Hira. "She *is* very talkative."

Mrs. Hakim laughs. "This is an advantage; you will see. She is not afraid to make mistakes, and that is how she will learn English even more quickly."

Mrs. Hakim exchanges thanks with Auntie and my

mother, then leaves us with Mrs. Fayad. After the glowing words Mrs. Hakim had for Hira, Mrs. Fayad looks sorry for whatever she is about to say.

"Bilal did a nice job, too," she says, looking like I didn't do a nice job at all. "He does have a solid base in English."

My mother nods.

"He will start the year as a level 2 ESL student."

My mother's smile fades, and I wish *I* could fade right into the carpet. Hira slips her hand into mine. Even she feels bad for me.

Mrs. Fayad continues in Urdu: "Bilal will receive special instruction from an ESL teacher. He'll spend most of his time in his fifth-grade class, but he'll meet with the ESL teacher for anywhere from sixty to ninety minutes each day, depending on how quickly he progresses."

Sixty to ninety minutes? A day?

I have studied English four more years than Hira has, yet I am the one who needs extra help? I know none of this is Hira's fault. But when she looks up at me with a sad face, I turn away.

My mother thanks Mrs. Fayad and nudges me to do the same. "Thank you," I mumble, slipping my hand from Hira's and putting both hands in my pockets. But thanks for what? For proving my little sister is better at English than I am? We leave the room and head back down the hall in silence.

You take English for five years and you think you know something, but then you come to a place where people speak a different kind of English, and you realize you know nothing.

Nine

Every morning after saying all the words in the *Fajr* prayer, I ask Allah for this to be the day that Baba tells us he is coming to America. For the last forty-five days, the answer has been "Not yet."

These last few weeks have been a blur of baseball camp, more new English words, and hanging out at the pool with the guys. I don't run into Jordan at the pool again, and I wonder if maybe she has made some non-baseball friends. I hope so.

The best thing about baseball camp is that tomorrow is the last day.

When Jalaal told me baseball is kind of like cricket, he was wrong. Sure, baseball has a bat and a ball, but even those are different in cricket. After six long weeks of camp, I still can't hit a ball with a round bat. I mean, I can hit it; I just can't hit the ball where it is supposed to go. Jalaal said I should give it time, but six weeks is time enough.

If Mudassar ever comes to America to visit, this is the baseball advice I will give him:

1. Baseball players only bat one at a time. If you ask where the second batter is, people will look at you funny.
2. If you get a hit, do not carry your bat when you run around the bases.
3. If you hit the ball and it pops up and over the line behind home plate, you do not earn four runs for your team. In fact, this is called a *foul ball*, and it is not a good thing. If this happens to you, do not jump and cheer and pump your fist in the air. Just get ready to bat again.
4. Home runs are worth four points at the most, and only if the bases are loaded. If someone hits a home run with the bases loaded, do not high-five everyone as they cross home plate, and yell, "Six points for us!"

The only thing I am okay at is pitching.

But Jordan is better. She is also better at hitting the ball than I am. Then again, so is everyone else.

"Hey, Bilal!" I turn to see Akash running across the field. He catches up to me, breathing hard, and jabs his thumb over his shoulder toward the gym doors. "Why didn't you sign up? Travel tryouts are tomorrow."

I shake my head. "I would not make the team anyway."

I have had enough humiliation for one summer, thank you very much. I don't need to try out for a travel baseball team to remind everyone how much I stink at this sport. I just want to forget all about baseball.

"Aw, come on, man." Akash spits onto the grass. "You're just getting used to the rules. And batting. And, you know, catching with a glove."

There is nothing I can say to that.

"We need a good pitcher." Akash raises his eyebrows, waiting for me to speak.

"Thank you, Akash. But Jordan will make your team. Everyone knows she is the best pitcher." I look behind me to make sure Henry isn't nearby, and lower my voice just in case. "She can also bat better than most everyone else."

Akash shakes his head. "Girls don't play baseball. Softball, sure. Baseball? No way." He shrugs. "Look, Bilal, last year we went all the way to the state finals down in Richmond. We lost to some team from Loudoun County."

I have no idea where these places are, but I do know having me on their team will not help them win. I would be fine with pitching, if only I didn't have to bat. Coach Matt already explained that all players have to bat, even the pitcher. It's the rule.

Jalaal saves me from more conversation when he shouts my name from the parking lot, waving both hands over his head.

Akash glances at Jalaal and then turns back to me. "Will you at least think about it?"

"Okay," I say, but the only thing I am thinking about is how I am not going to try out.

Akash seems satisfied with my answer, and we agree to meet tomorrow morning at the field.

I head over toward Jalaal, relief flowing through me with

64

every step. After tomorrow, the last day of camp, I won't have to pick up another baseball bat as long as I live.

"Hey, little buddy. *Vámonos?*" Jalaal claps his hand on my shoulder.

"*Vámonos.*" I grin at this strange, new English word.

Jalaal has a plan to speak to me in English so I can learn more before school starts. So far he speaks to me mostly in English and I answer him mostly in Urdu, especially when I'm tired. Thinking in English hurts my brain after a while. I know Jalaal is trying to be helpful, but I also think maybe he doesn't feel comfortable speaking Urdu anymore—kind of like a favorite T-shirt you used to wear everywhere, even to bed, and now it just doesn't fit.

We throw our bags into the back, and Jalaal starts the car. "You ready for tomorrow?"

I nod. Ready for camp to be over.

Jalaal slows the car at a stop sign and then rolls through the empty intersection. "We can throw some pitches in the backyard later, if you want."

"Sounds good." As long as we just pitch—no batting.

"You'll blow them away tomorrow, Bilal."

I look at Jalaal. "Blow who away?"

"The competition, my friend. No doubt you'll make the team."

"What? But I didn't write my name down," I say.

His smile returns. "Don't worry—I signed you up."

"Jalaal!"

His eyes open wide with pretend innocence. "What?"

"I didn't sign up on purpose."

"Bilal, you're kidding. You're an amazing pitcher."

But I'm also amazingly bad at batting. I guess Jalaal knows, because he says, "We'll work on the batting. You'll be fine.

"The travel team is called the Fairfax Cardinals, but they're opening up a developmental team this year, too."

"Cardinals?"

"They're birds." Jalaal glances out his side window. "I don't see any now, but they're red—at least the males are. The females are brown."

Birds don't sound like a very ferocious mascot. But I think I have seen the kind of bird that Jalaal is talking about—they like to eat from Auntie's bird feeder in the backyard.

"What is the developmental team?"

Jalaal looks both ways before cruising through another stop sign. "The developmental team works more on basic skills. No official games, only scrimmages—kind of like practice games that don't count."

Games that don't count? I just want to play cricket, and that is all.

I roll down the window and prop my elbow in the open space, leaning my head against my hand. The houses gliding by remind me of the plastic pieces in the Monopoly game we played after dinner last night—each house looks the same, except for their color. Every garden is neat and trim, and I'll bet someone sweeps the streets every morning, because there isn't any trash. No one beeps their horn or passes anyone on these streets, which are wide enough for four cars. Almost everyone stops at the stop signs, even when no cars are coming. A man and his daughter hose off their already-clean car. There are no donkeys pulling carts or skinny, stray dogs sniffing for food— these American dogs have collars and leashes and families.

"Bilal?" Jalaal sounds concerned. "You okay?"

I shrug, and Jalaal sighs.

"I got you," he says. "I missed Pakistan at first, too. But you'll get used to it here."

I am not so sure I will ever get used to America.

"And hey, once you make the team, you'll get to know all the guys even better."

I know he's right, but making friends in English is exhausting. I pretend to understand everything they say, but they talk too fast, use words I don't know, and use words I do know in ways I don't understand. At least Jalaal mixes in some Urdu every once in a while, and he teaches me new English words.

"Besides," he says, "baseball is a totally American sport. It'll help you fit in."

I'm not sure I want to fit in. I mean, I do, but I don't. If I become American, will I still be Pakistani?

Jalaal glances in the rearview mirror. "In a few months, you'll be as American as mom, baseball, and apple pie."

"What?"

Jalaal laughs at the look on my face. "It's a saying. If something is really American, they say it's like mom, baseball, and apple pie."

I have never tried apple pie, but why are moms so American? Moms are everywhere, including Pakistan.

Jalaal keeps glancing my way; I can tell he is worried about me. I smile so he won't worry, and also so he'll stop looking at me and watch the road.

Jalaal turns onto our street—his street—and that's when we see Olivia heading down her driveway, toward a Jeep where some other kids are waiting.

Olivia's face brightens when she sees us. I wave and call, "Hi, Olivia!" out the window.

Olivia ducks her head into the Jeep, says something to the driver, then crosses the lawn. Jalaal is out of the car before I even unbuckle my seat belt.

"Hey, Jalaal." Olivia smiles and tucks some hair behind her ear. "We're going to the lake for a swim. Want to come?"

I wonder for a second if Jalaal even heard her, because he's standing there looking like he's forgotten how to speak.

Olivia gives my shoulder a gentle punch. "Hey, Bilal. How's baseball camp going?"

I tilt my head while I think of how to answer. "The last day is tomorrow."

She smiles. "That bad, huh?"

I like Olivia.

The Jeep's horn beeps twice. Olivia looks back, holds up her index finger, then turns back to Jalaal. "So do you want to come with us?"

Jalaal finds his voice. "Sounds fun—but I can't."

The light in Olivia's eyes dims. "Okay. Maybe another time."

Jalaal shoves his hands into his front pockets, and now he and Olivia look like drooping mirror images of each other. "Sure. Another time."

Olivia takes a deep breath. "Okay." She smiles at me. "See you guys around."

Before I can wave, she's halfway to the Jeep. The boy in the driver's seat starts the engine, and they back out of the driveway. Jalaal looks like that Jeep is dragging his heart right down the street with Olivia. I reach up and clap my hand on his shoulder, like he does to me when he knows I'm feeling down.

It seems to work, because he blinks and opens the back door of the car. We pull out our baseball bags and lug them into the garage before heading into the kitchen.

Auntie is waiting for us with tea. "Boys!" She smiles.

From the living room my mother's voice mixes with Hira's laughter and another girl's voice that's kind of familiar. "Bilal?" my mother calls. "Is that you?"

I stride into the living room and stop short.

There on the couch, talking to Hira, is Jordan.

Ten

What surprises me most is Jordan's hair. I've only ever seen it in a dark, curly ponytail, or tucked up inside her cap. But now her hair is loose, almost touching her shoulders. She definitely has that thing Jalaal calls *hat head*.

Eventually I find my voice. "Why you are here?"

My mother smiles but says, "Bilal! Don't be rude." Thankfully, she says this in Urdu, which I assume Jordan does not understand.

Until Hira translates: "My mother says Bilal is being rude." My sister shakes her head, as if the burden of having a rude brother is just too much to bear.

"Hira," my mother whispers, and gives her a look that stops Hira's head-shaking.

Jordan stands, her face red. "I have to go, actually."

I know I should say something, but I can't stop staring at her red face. I mean, it really is red. I've never seen a face change colors that quickly.

My mother clears her throat. "Bilal, why don't you offer our guest some more tea?"

I reach out to take Jordan's almost-full cup.

"Uh, no thank you." Jordan hands over the tea. "I really need to get home."

She picks up my Nationals cap from the coffee table. "This was sitting on the bench when Uncle—er, Coach—Matt and Kyle were bringing in the equipment. I thought you might need it for tomorrow."

"Oh, thank you." I hadn't even realized I'd left it behind. I step forward and take it from her.

Jordan thanks my mom for the tea, smiles at Hira, and heads for the door.

Humza's cry from upstairs announces his nap is over, and Ammi excuses herself. Before leaving the room, she mouths to me, "Walk her to the door."

All the way down the hall, I try to think of something to say to Jordan. After that day at the pool last month, she keeps to herself at baseball camp. I don't think the guys even notice. They are too busy avoiding her.

She must be trying out for a travel softball team, so I say, "Good luck with the trying out."

Or should I have said *tryouts*? While I am debating this, she smiles and looks surprised.

"Thanks, Bilal." She steps onto the porch and reaches for her bat and glove, which are leaning against the brick wall of the house. "At first I thought I'd hold on to your cap until to-morrow, but then I wondered if it's your lucky charm."

"Lucky charm?"

She shrugs, threading her bat through her cap and glove

71

before resting it on her shoulder. "If it's a lucky cap, I figured you'd want it back."

I don't know the word *charm*, but she obviously realizes I need lots of luck.

She nods. "See you tomorrow, then."

"Oh, I am not trying out."

Her eyebrows rise. "But I saw your name on the list."

I shrug. "Jalaal signed me up. But I will not make the team."

"How do you know? You're a great pitcher."

"Thank you. But even you say I need luck."

She shakes her head, sending her curls bobbing. "We all could use some luck."

Maybe, but Jordan needs a lot less luck than I do.

"Anyway, you should think about it." Jordan turns and heads toward the sidewalk, her glove and cap swinging from the bat over her shoulder.

She's halfway down the front walk when she turns and comes back. "So do you want to practice pitching sometime?"

Her question catches me by surprise. Does she mean practice with her?

When I don't answer right away, two bright spots of red appear on her cheeks and she puts her cap back on over her curls. "I know your cousin practices with you, and I've got Uncle Matt. But since we're both new . . . just thought I'd ask."

While I try to figure out the right words to say, she props one fist on her hip.

Why does she want to practice baseball anyway, when Akash says she is going to play softball? Maybe she thinks I need help, which is right. Maybe she just likes to play, and Coach Matt is too busy to practice with her.

72

I am about to say that I'll practice with her when Hira's voice drifts down the hall from the living room: "Baba!"

I step back inside. In Urdu, I call, "Tell Baba I want to talk, too!"

Jordan shifts from one foot to the other. "Or there are these batting cages, if you haven't been."

Ammi swoops down the stairs with Humza. "Yes, Humza—it's Baba!" She hurries down the hall and disappears into the living room.

Jordan stands on tiptoe to see what's happening behind me, but I know she didn't understand Ammi's Urdu words.

"I must go." I close the door and then open it again quickly, because I know I seem rude. "Sorry!" I close the door again and race into the living room.

Hira leans toward the computer, arms around Humza, giggling and nodding as Baba smiles from the screen. "That's right, Baba—camping. It's what Girl Scouts do. Ammi says I have to be older first, so I thought of a great idea! I'm going to camp in the backyard in a tent all night long with my new friend, Lizzie. We'll bring a Girl Scout snack called trail mix so we won't get hungry, and we have sleeping bags . . ."

Even though Humza keeps crawling up to the screen to give Baba kisses, Hira still manages to tell Baba everything there is to know about Girl Scouts. Finally Ammi ushers them out of the room so I can have my turn.

Baba smiles. "I have a Karachi memory for you, Bilal."

I lean in. "What is it?"

He holds up his palm to reveal a fluffy, bright blue chick. It peeps and takes a few steps before cocking its head.

"You're going to the farm!" I wish I could go with him.

Every time we visit the wheat farm where my grandmother grew up, we buy a chick from a street vendor and take it with us. Baba figures it's ten rupees well spent, and Daddo's brother is always happy to add a new member to the chicken coop. By the time the chick loses its dyed fluff, it will look like all the rest of the chickens.

Baba gently places the chick back into the box. "Okay, now it is your turn."

I tell Baba about how the power only goes off here when you turn it off.

"Remarkable," Baba says. "And here we still do not have enough electricity to go around." He shakes his head before changing the subject. "Tomorrow is your last day of baseball camp, Bilal *jaan*."

I sigh. "Well, it is not exactly my final last day."

Baba raises an eyebrow. "Oh?"

"Jalaal signed me up for tryouts—a team called the Fairfax Cardinals."

I explain to Baba what a cardinal is, because we don't have them in Pakistan. Baba's eyes crinkle on the sides when he smiles. "So my son will play on an American baseball team."

He sounds so proud. Good thing he has never seen me actually play.

"It's not like that, Baba. Jalaal wants me to try out, but I don't know if I want to." I rest my chin in one hand. "Baseball is hard—too different from cricket."

"Of course it is hard; it is something new. It is a challenge, but you can do it. Before long, you will be the best Cardinal of all—I am sure of it."

I think of all the times Baba practiced cricket with me until

74

I became strong and fast and finally held the Karachi youth record for most wickets taken. Now I am learning a whole new game, an American game without any wickets—no sticks to knock over at home plate.

Baba's shoulders rise, followed by a sigh. "I know it is not easy, Bilal *jaan*."

Baba is not talking about baseball.

"Your mother says you are being strong. I am proud of you."

I don't know what to say, because I have done nothing to make Baba proud. I think of all the times I haven't tried my best at baseball camp because I've been afraid of making a fool of myself.

"When are you coming, Baba?"

"I am not sure yet. Soon, I hope. And when I do come, I promise I will be there to see you play on the team of Cardinals."

I sit up straight. "You promise?"

"I promise, Bilal. *Inshallah*."

If Allah wills it.

I hope Allah knows that first He will have to help me make the team. And then I hope He knows baseball season ends in November, so He will have to get Baba here before then.

# Eleven

"So here's the thing," Akash says as we walk out to the field the next morning. "You're one of the fastest throwers out there, Bilal. When you're up at bat, just keep your eye on the ball. You'll be fine."

I definitely don't feel fine. There must be at least forty kids sitting out there on the bleachers.

When we reach the group, Akash drops his bag at his feet. "What is *she* doing here?"

I know who he's talking about even before I spot Jordan's curly ponytail sticking out of her baseball cap.

Akash lets out a long breath. "Girls don't try out for boys' travel baseball teams."

Apparently they do. I do not say this to Akash.

"Okay, folks!" Coach Matt claps his hand on the shoulder of a man who can't be much taller than I am. "Some of you worked with Coach Pablo last year on the travel team." A few kids murmur and nod.

Coach Pablo's dark blue shorts and white camp T-shirt look like the clean, crisp "after" from a laundry soap commercial, with Coach Matt's rumpled clothes as the "before." Coach Pablo raises his cap. "Gentlemen."

Jordan crosses her arms. Coach Pablo must notice, because he clears his throat and tries again. "Er, ladies and gentlemen."

Coach Matt continues: "Our high school helpers, Kyle and Jalaal, will distribute your pinnies. Reds and greens, you'll be with Jalaal and me on the lower field. Yellows and blues go with Coach Pablo and Kyle on the upper diamond."

In a flurry of arms and colorful mesh, everyone slips on their pinnies and moves into groups. I poke my head through a yellow pinnie, but no one I know is wearing yellow. At least Akash and Jordan have blue pinnies, so they'll be in Coach Pablo's group with me.

When we get to the dugout, Coach Pablo squints at us from underneath the shade of his cap, like he is sizing us up. I swallow.

"Okay, players. Here is how it is going to work."

His English is a little different from the way Coach Matt talks; slower and easier to understand.

"This morning everyone will have several chances up at bat. Kyle will play catcher, and I will pitch through the first cycle until everyone has batted."

Cycle?

"Then we take a water break, and I will rotate some of you in as pitchers."

Rotate?

"Once everyone has batted a second time, we will let you know who makes the cut."

We have to cut something?

Coach Pablo is not so easy to understand after all.

"Yellow team, you're up at bat." Coach Pablo checks something off on his clipboard, and my heart sinks to my ankles. We're batting first? Why couldn't we start out on the field? I go to the very end of the line, behind a boy with the number ten on the back of his T-shirt. I recognize his face from camp, but I don't remember his name. Number Ten turns and says, "Wait 'til you see this guy swing."

A tall boy strides over to home plate like he can't wait to get started. He grips the bat with one hand, flexes his fingers on the other, then switches hands and repeats. He taps home plate with the toe of each cleat, then plants his feet in the dirt. After taking a few practice swings, he thumps home base with his bat three times, releasing a cloud of red dust. Pulling the bat over his shoulder, he nods at Coach Pablo.

Number Ten whispers, "Nate's good-luck ritual works every time. Watch this."

Coach Pablo lets the ball fly, and sure enough, Nate sends it back, clear over second base. The players in the outfield scramble for the ball while Nate sails around one base after the other until he rounds third on his way back home.

Kyle springs up from his catcher position, lifts his face mask, and whistles. "That kid sure can run."

Nate performs a spectacular slide into home plate even though the ball isn't anywhere near him.

Kyle pats him on the shoulder. "That was epic, Nate."

"Thanks, man." Nate grins at Kyle, then shrugs like making a home run is no big deal. Nate reminds me of myself during cricket tryouts—confident I would make the top team. Nate brushes past the next kid, Aiden, who mutters to himself and takes so many deep breaths that I start to worry he'll pass out. There were kids like Aiden on my cricket team, but I never thought to encourage them during tryouts. Now I wish I had.

"You got this, Aiden," Kyle says before squatting into catcher position.

Aiden takes his helmet off, turns it over in his hands, puts it on, takes it off, and puts it on again. He tosses his bat from one hand to the other three times, draws a line in the dirt with his toe, then grips the bat.

Number Ten whispers, "Aiden's ritual never works."

Coach Pablo pitches. Aiden swings—and misses.

"Strike one!" Kyle calls, but he sounds sorry about it. Aiden cringes.

Number Ten keeps his voice low. "He tries all these new lucky moves, but it doesn't work that way." He shakes his head.

"What is the good way?" I ask.

Number Ten sighs. "You can't just make up any old good-luck ritual, you know?"

I don't know, but I nod anyway.

"I mean, do you think Joe DiMaggio randomly invented his good-luck routines?" Number Ten shakes his head. "Man, they were inspired."

I shake my head, too, but I have no idea who Joe Di . . . whatever-his-name-is is. Did Omar Khan ever have a lucky ritual before cricket matches? Maybe Baba will remember from his cricket-playing days with Omar Khan.

"Strike two!" Kyle calls.

I wince—partly for Aiden and partly for myself, because I know I won't do any better. This time Aiden doesn't do any of

79

his lucky movements. He just stands there, bat over his shoulder. He might even be praying, judging by the way his lips are moving.

Coach Pablo tosses the ball underhand this time. It traces a lazy upward arc, falling right where Aiden can't miss it. Ball and bat connect with a hollow thunk. Aiden drops the bat and takes off toward first base like he is being chased by a mad rhinoceros. The ball rolls a slow path toward Coach Pablo. He scoops it up, waits a few seconds for Aiden to reach Jordan at first base, and then signals to Number Ten.

Kyle nods. "You got this, Jack."

Jack—now I remember Number Ten's name. From all Jack's talk about good-luck rituals, I should have known he'd have one of his own. He jogs clockwise around home plate, reverses direction and jogs around once more. He spins his bat like a baton, passing it from one hand to the other. It seems like he won't ever stop until Coach Pablo yells, "Jack! You are batting today, yes?"

Could Jack choose to bat tomorrow, instead? Could I?

But Jack doesn't choose tomorrow; he chooses today. He barely catches his spinning bat, almost dropping it before holding it high over his shoulder. He nods.

Jack hits the pitch on his first swing. Flinging his bat aside, he sprints toward first base while the ball rolls straight to third. Jack is already past first and heading for second when the kid on third throws the ball like a bullet to second. The kid on second catches it right before Jack slides into him.

"Out!"

Jack picks himself up and brushes off the seat of his pants, shaking his head.

Kyle calls, "Nice, Jack!" He adjusts his face mask as he squats down for the next pitch. Kyle shakes his head. "Risky, though," he says, keeping his voice low. "He should have stayed on first."

I wouldn't know, because I have never been on first. Or second. Or third. And I'm only ever on the home base when I'm batting.

"You're up, Bilal," Coach Pablo calls. I silently command my stomach to stop flip-flopping as I hurry over and grab a bat. When I walk around to the lefty side of home base, Coach Pablo shifts back a step. I position my feet and raise my bat, hoping no one notices that it's trembling. Before I steady myself, Coach Pablo pitches the ball. I am not ready, but I swing anyway.

Too soon. My bat whooshes into nothing a half second before the ball speeds past my nose and thwacks into Kyle's glove.

I swallow, and reposition my feet.

Kyle's voice comes from behind me. "That was just a warm-up. You got this, Bilal."

I take a shaky breath. I didn't have a lucky ritual in cricket. But when Baba was in the stands, he would catch my eye and pat his heart twice. I would pat my heart, too. It wasn't for luck, really—it was his way of saying, "I love watching you play cricket," and it was my way of saying back, "Thank you for being here."

I adjust my wobbly helmet. Maybe patting my heart twice will bring me luck. So I do it—two quick pats so no one will notice—then I lift my bat high. I am ready.

When the ball leaves Coach Pablo's hand this time, I don't take my eyes off it for even half a second. I remember what

Jalaal told me about waiting until the ball is in my hitting zone, so I wait ... wait ... swing! I feel the crack of the bat vibrate from my fingers clear up to my elbows. I don't stop to see where the ball goes; I just run. I'm halfway to first base when I remember I'm still clutching the bat. I toss it aside and hear it clatter to the ground. Legs pumping, arms swinging, I don't see Jordan waving me back until I'm almost to first.

"Bilal!" Coach Pablo calls. I skid to a stop in a cloud of dirt and turn to see Kyle waving both arms. "Foul ball!"

No one laughs, but the players on the field suddenly find something very interesting on the ground right behind them.

I trudge back toward home base, swiping my bat off the ground along the way.

"Don't sweat it, Bilal. Wait a half second longer to swing." Kyle punches his glove. "This one's yours, buddy."

"*Inshallah*," I say automatically, forgetting Kyle doesn't know what this means. *If Allah wills it.*

Judging from the last six weeks of camp, I don't think me playing baseball is Allah's will. But it *is* Baba's will. If baseball can get Baba here sooner, then I have to make the Cardinals.

I decide to try the double pat again, but this time I don't hide it. I pat my heart twice, the way I would if Baba were in the stands.

I get into position and nod at Coach Pablo. He pulls his elbow back, knee raised, then launches the ball.

I force myself to wait—not yet ... not yet—now! My shoulders swivel, my body twists, and *crack!* I drop my bat and run. I can almost see Daddo in the stands, tiny next to my towering Baba, cheering louder than even the men. Jordan shouts something from first base, her glove high, face tipped toward the sun. I speed toward her—five meters, four, three, two—she leaps, arm stretched to the sky. The ball whacks into the pocket of her glove before her heel lands back on base half a second before my foot slams into first in a cloud of red dust.

"Out!" Coach Pablo calls.

Jordan offers a hand to help me up. The guys all stare.

I turn, pretending not to see her hand as I stand and brush the dirt from my knees.

"Nice hit, Bilal," she says, tossing the ball back to Coach.

I nod my thanks, but my heart is not thankful. I couldn't even get to first base. I think the double-heart pat is only lucky when there are two hearts and two hands and Baba is there in the stands.

✦   ✦   ✦

Finally Allah must hear my baseball prayers: not one ball flies my way the whole time I am stuck in the outfield.

Jordan hits a double and a home run. The boys from camp say she bats like a girl. But if batting like a girl means getting bases, I wouldn't mind batting like a girl. I try to imagine how I would feel if a girl joined my cricket team back home. Then I imagine what it would be like to play cricket with a girl who is better than me. And that is how I start to understand how the other boys feel.

After everyone has batted and we take a water break, Coach Pablo tosses me the ball. "Coach Matt tells me you're a southpaw pitcher."

I do not know what a southpaw is, so I just say, "I like to pitch."

He claps me on the shoulder. "Let's see what you've got."

Before I can tell him that I haven't got anything, Coach Pablo waves Jordan over.

"Your uncle said I should see you pitch."

Jordan looks down, like she's trying to hide the proud smile tugging at the corners of her mouth.

"I'm giving each of you a chance on the bump." He nods and strides toward the dugout.

"The bump?"

I don't realize I've said this out loud until Jordan answers me, nodding toward the pitching mound. "He's letting us both pitch." She says it like this is a common question instead of a stupid one, and for that I am grateful.

The rest of the morning flies by, but that's because there isn't as much running this time around—Jordan strikes out three kids (including me, of course), and I strike out two (not including Jordan, of course).

And then it's time to find out who is a Cardinal and who is not.

A honking sound comes from the sky as a flock of fat, brown geese fly in a V over our heads. Jalaal says they are called *Canada geese*, so I wonder what they are doing here in America. As the geese fly past, Coach Matt roars with laughter and points to Coach Pablo's dark blue cap, where a greenish-white stain runs across the white *NY* on the front. Coach Pablo takes off his cap and shakes his fist at the geese, yelling a word I have never heard followed by "Red Sox fans!" I don't understand this, but everyone laughs, so I laugh, too. It must have something to do with the pair of red socks on the front of Coach Matt's blue cap.

Coach Pablo wipes off his hat with a towel as Coach Matt calls, "Listen up, players!"

Voices lower to whispers, then fade to silence, broken only by the occasional cracking sound of a plastic cap on a new bottle of Gatorade.

"We appreciate the effort you've made out here today, each and every one of you."

Coach Pablo nods a sad kind of nod that comes when there's bad news with good. He clears his throat. "If we call your name, it means you have made the cut."

I feel like I might lose the cereal and toast I had for breakfast. Baba promised he would come to see me play, and he has never once broken a promise to me. I have to make the Cardinals.

Coach Matt swats an invisible bug with his clipboard. "If you are not on our list today, we hope you'll sign up for our fall developmental program."

Henry groans and rests his forehead on his knees. Akash takes in a deep breath and lets it out through puffed cheeks.

As Coach Matt reads each name, kids jump up like popcorn, whooping, high-fiving, fist-bumping.

Until Jordan's name is called.

I start clapping, then stop when I realize I am the only one. Everyone else is silent.

More names are read, the applause starts up again, and Jordan keeps her head down.

Akash is called, and I add my own high five. But I can't stop glancing over at Jordan, hoping someone sitting near her will at least offer a smile. No one even looks at her.

"That's it for today, everyone." Coach Matt tucks his clipboard under his arm. My chance to make the Cardinals is gone.

Henry hangs his head. I really thought he would make the team.

Coach Pablo holds up a stack of papers. "Anyone interested in the developmental team can pick up a flyer on your way out."

Akash looks at his cleats like he doesn't know what to say to Henry and me. I don't blame him.

"Congratulations," I offer, and that seems to make him feel even worse.

Akash shakes his head. "I'm sorry, man." He friendship-punches my shoulder, but it doesn't help. He gives Henry a friendship-punch, too, but Henry just shakes his head.

As I head over to get my bag, Coach Matt stops me. "Can I talk to you a moment, son?" Coach Matt hands me a flyer. "We'd love to work with you this fall, Bilal—you and that left pitching arm of yours."

I take the flyer, but I am not sure what he means. "I can be a Cardinal?"

"Well, not exactly. Not yet, anyway." Coach Matt folds his arms. "What I mean is, we'd like you to train with the developmental team. Your pitching is definitely good enough to make the Cardinals. We just need to get your batting up to par."

Coach Matt points to a website address at the bottom of the flyer. "Jalaal can help you sign up, but if you or your parents have any questions, let me know."

He claps me on the shoulder before striding away to talk to another kid. I stand there for a minute more, trying to imagine how I'll tell Baba that I didn't make the team.

"Bilal, you coming?" Akash is waiting for me, his bag slung over his shoulder.

I gather my equipment and we catch up to Henry. I am about to tell the guys what Coach Matt said when I see the developmental team flyer clutched in Henry's hand.

Henry shakes his head. "I can't believe I didn't make the team." He glares at Jordan from across the field.

"It's not fair," Akash says, kicking a patch of dirt.

Henry spits. "I should've known. She's Coach Matt's niece."

Akash narrows his eyes. "Yeah, nepotism."

Henry says what I'm thinking: "Nepa-what?"

"*Nepotism*. Meaning her uncle's the head coach, so she made the team."

I stand there shaking my head like I can't believe Jordan is a Cardinal instead of Henry.

But the truth is, I can believe it.

Even so, I decide I won't tell Baba about Jordan at all. Maybe by the time he gets here and sees me play, I'll be the one pitching for the Cardinals instead of her.

Twelve

I am not hungry for breakfast on my first day of school. I pick chunks of tomato from my omelet, slip them under my toast, and push bits of egg around my plate. During my *Fajr* prayer this morning, I prayed that a monsoon would close school today.

"School bus in ten minutes!" Auntie calls from upstairs.

I guess that prayer won't be answered today.

I take my plate to the sink and rinse it, stuffing my whole omelet down the garbage disposal.

For the tenth time since last night, I check my backpack. It's stuffed with notebooks and pencils and highlighters and markers and a bunch of other things I have never needed for school before, like plastic zip bags and disinfectant wipes. A letter came last week saying that Mrs. Wu will be my teacher, which is good. But Akash and Henry have a different teacher, which is not good; I won't have anyone to ask what I am supposed to do with zip bags and disinfectant wipes.

Auntie whooshes down the stairs, the hem of her jade *shalwar kameez* fluttering behind her. "Off we go!" She claps her hands.

I file out the door behind Auntie, Hira, and Ammi, who pushes Humza in his stroller. My sister runs to catch up to Lizzie, swinging her new American backpack over her shoulder.

As soon as we join the crowd of kids and parents, a little girl in a soccer T-shirt squeals, "Here comes the bus!" A very tall boy herds the little kids into line. When he turns, I see that he's wearing a neon-yellow belt diagonally across his chest, complete with a silver badge.

The other parents snap photos with their phones, and so do Ammi and Auntie.

"Smile!" Ammi calls, and I feel like melting into the sidewalk. If my Karachi classmates were here, we'd make silly faces or strike funny poses. It's just not as fun by yourself. I only smile for real when my mother says, "We'll send this one to Baba."

Jordan stands last in line, right behind me. She whisper-yells, "Mom! I'm too old for this. Honestly."

I don't turn, but I hear her mother whisper back, "Come on, honey—just one photo. We'll email it to your dad."

I don't know if Jordan smiles or not, but her mom takes a picture anyway and steps back with the other parents.

I turn to ask Jordan about her dad. Her arms are crossed and she kicks a pebble into the grass behind her. Maybe I'll ask about her dad another time.

The bus is crowded, with three to a seat. It smells like

exhaust fumes and vinyl seats. As we shuffle down the aisle, I spot Henry, Akash, and another kid sitting together. Akash sits near the aisle and high-fives me as I walk past. I wish there were space for me. Hira and Lizzie sit with another kid, and I grab the very last empty seat at the back.

As soon as I sit down, Jordan slides next to me.

"Hey." She pulls off her backpack and sets it on her lap.

"Hello." I set my backpack on my lap, too.

Akash catches my eye. He grins, then turns back and leans in to say something to Henry and the other boy. They all burst into laughter.

I sink down into my seat. It's not my fault I'm sitting with a girl, and it's not Jordan's fault she's sitting with me.

Either Jordan is oblivious to Henry's glares or she doesn't care. "So are you nervous?"

"A little bit, yes." And not just about school. I glance over at the guys. "You are nervous?" I ask.

"Nah." Jordan shrugs. "I've done this before." She unzips and zips the front pocket of her backpack.

I wish Henry would stop looking back here. I can't shake the feeling that the three of them are talking about me. And maybe Jordan. Probably both of us.

"Well?" Jordan asks.

I blink. Did she just ask me a question?

Jordan opens her mouth as if she is going to repeat whatever she said, but then she glances over at the guys, who are still snickering. She scowls, hugs her backpack tighter, then unzips it and pulls out a book. She opens to a bookmarked page and starts reading. When I try to look at the words on the bumpy bus, my stomach turns over.

I lean against the window, watching neat rows of houses roll by. In Karachi, Baba always drove me to school, and it was one of my favorite times of the day. The clatter of voices bouncing off the school bus walls is nothing like the quiet hum of Baba's car. The bus doesn't make any more stops after mine, and we're pulling up in front of the school before I am ready.

Jordan hops up from the seat as the bus lurches to a stop. By the time the brakes squeak and sigh and the door swings open, she's already four people ahead of me in line. Henry and Akash file off the bus right in front of her, without looking back. When I finally step onto the sidewalk, only Akash is waiting for me.

I want to thank him for waiting and to ask why Henry looked so mad at me, but it is too loud and too crowded, and anyway I think I already know. But it is not my fault that Jordan made the Cardinals instead of Henry or that Jordan sat next to me on the only empty seat on the bus.

I try to keep up with Akash as he weaves his way through the throng of kids and into the cafeteria. Most kids are seated at long tables, talking to friends. Others gather near the walls, laughing and fist-bumping and friendship-punching.

Akash and I finally find Henry standing near the back of the cafeteria with a group of boys. Akash introduces me to the others, but he says their names so fast I don't catch most of them.

Although I am standing with these boys, I am not part of their group. They talk and joke around me, but I don't understand everything they say. I see Jordan standing with her book, leaning against the white tile wall. She is alone; I am with a group of kids. But I am the one who feels lonely.

There's Hira chatting with Lizzie and two other little girls. I look away; I am not *that* desperate for company.

It feels like forever before a tone sounds over the loudspeaker and everyone starts herding themselves out of the double doors. I quickly lose sight of Akash. I head for the stairs and make my way to room twenty-five.

Mrs. Wu greets me at the door, and I am surprised to see I am the first one here. I was never the first one to class back home. Mudassar and I always waited until the last possible moment before rushing through the door and sliding into our seats. My new classmates spill into the room a few seconds after me.

"Welcome, boys and girls!" Mrs. Wu says. "Please read the morning message and settle in."

A projector lights up a whiteboard with a message:

Good Morning and Welcome to Fifth Grade!
1. **Unpack your backpack.**
2. **Put your supplies inside your desk.**
3. **Place your backpack in your cubby.**
4. **Begin the icebreaker on your desk.**

I pull my supplies from my backpack one by one, buying time until I can figure out what a cubby is. One girl dumps her school supplies onto her desk and brings her empty backpack to some open cupboards. I head back, too, and find a hook for my backpack next to my name.

Now for the icebreaker. I don't know what that is, but there is a piece of paper on my desk with sixteen squares and some writing. Each square has a question like *What is your favorite subject?* or *How many siblings do you have?*

I take a breath and nod. I know enough English to do this. I fill in my answers until I get to the "favorite sport" box. I start to write *baseball*, but then I wonder if Mrs. Wu has heard of cricket. Maybe she will know it is a game and not a bug. I write it down. For my favorite subject, I write "English" so Mrs. Wu will know I have studied English, and maybe I won't have to do the ESL class. My favorite food is *jalebi*. Thinking about the warm, crispy sweetness of the saffron orange spirals makes me wish I'd finished my breakfast. I blink and look back at my paper. Favorite vacation spot? Margalla Hills National Park at the foot of the mountains in Islamabad. Favorite summer memory? Talking to Baba on Skype.

I finally put down my pencil and look up to find Jordan sitting across from me, moving her pencil across her paper. I'd been so focused on my answers that I hadn't even realized she'd come in. I feel sorry for not talking to her very much on the bus. I think about saying something to her now, but I don't want to get in trouble with the teacher on the very first day of school.

Mrs. Wu taps something on her laptop, and the image on the whiteboard changes from the morning work directions to a video of two kids sitting behind a big desk.

"Goooood morning, Panthers, and welcome to the first day of school!" they say in unison. They explain that this is the *Good Morning Panthers* news show, or *GMP* for short. Then they tell us to rise for something I don't understand. Everyone puts down their pencils, stands, and recites the same words all at the same time. They are about five seconds into these words when I realize everyone has a hand on their chest, so I do the same.

Then we sit back down and have something called a minute of silence, which I don't understand because we already had several minutes of silence before, while we were filling out the paper with the sixteen boxes.

The kids on TV tell us to have a great day, and then the screen goes to a picture of a fierce cat with long teeth and the words *Panther Pride*.

Mrs. Wu turns off the projector. "Okay, class, finish up your last answers, then we'll gather on the carpet for our first morning meeting of the year."

Kids wander over to the rug and sit cross-legged around the edge. In the center of the rug is a world map, with flags lining the perimeter. I look for the flag of Pakistan with its white star and crescent moon against a dark green background, but I do not see it. I pick a spot next to a boy with hair the color of a lemon.

Mrs. Wu reads the morning message and explains that the paper with the sixteen boxes is called an *icebreaker*. I am still not sure why, since I don't see how a piece of paper could break ice. Mrs. Wu then shows us how to do something called a *morning greeting*, which goes like this: you introduce yourself; you give a high five to the person on your left; that person says good morning to you; and you say it back. Then the person high-fives the next person, and so on, all the way around the circle.

I don't know how I will ever remember all of these names. I wonder if anyone else knows how to speak Urdu.

Then it's time for the icebreaker paper. Mrs. Wu tells us we are supposed to walk around with our paper and pencil and find someone whose answer matches one of ours. If we do, then we sign our name in the other person's box. I frown at my paper. No one's answers will match mine, except maybe the one about having a sister and a brother.

There is only one thing to do—change my answers. I could change cricket to baseball, but what about the vacation spot? I don't know where Americans go on vacation. And favorite summer memory? I could make something up—like going to the pool.

When everyone stands and starts to talk, I head back to my desk. Leaning over my paper, I flip my pencil to the eraser side, but Mrs. Wu calls out, "No changing answers, people! The object isn't to find a match for all the boxes—it's to get to know each other!"

It's obvious most kids already know each other anyway, because I hear things like, "Dylan—sign my box for favorite sport," when the kid called Dylan hasn't even seen the other kid's paper. The only person I know in this class is Jordan, but she's already exchanging papers with another girl who nods at something Jordan wrote.

Someone taps my shoulder, and I turn to find a tall boy with green eyes peering at me through his glasses. "Hey, what's your favorite sport?" he says.

I hold my paper to my chest. "What is yours?"

"Basketball." He points to his T-shirt, which has something about a tournament written across it. "We won our division last season."

I peek at my paper like I can't remember what I put down. "I did not write basketball," I say.

"Oh, okay." The boy shrugs. "What else you got?"

He turns his paper so I can scan his answers. I point to where he wrote that he has one brother and one sister.

"This one," I say.

We exchange papers, and he signs his name in the *How*

many siblings do you have? box. I do the same on his paper, scrawling my name quickly so we can switch back before he sees my other answers.

When I have my paper, I look at his name: José. I'm not sure how to pronounce it. He studies my signature. "What's your name?"

"Bilal," I say, vowing to write more clearly on the next person's paper. Although I probably won't find anyone whose answers match mine.

José nods. "Cool," he declares, and walks away.

As I suspected, I don't meet anyone else besides José who has the same answers I do. Jordan comes up to me, her paper filled with signatures.

I am so grateful to see a familiar face that I decide right then to apologize for not listening to her on the bus. But before I can open my mouth, she says, "What do you have left?"

She peers at my paper. "Fifteen?" Her voice gets the attention of a bunch of kids standing near us. They look over, then go back to talking and laughing and signing their names.

"Let me see that." Jordan grabs my paper. Before I can tell her I didn't write down *baseball* for my favorite sport, she's signing her name in one of my boxes—I can't see which one. She thrusts her paper at me, pointing to the box in the lower left-hand corner. "You can sign here."

I take her paper, and my eyes find the box she's pointing to—the only one without a signature: Favorite summer memory. Underneath, she's written, "Skype with my dad."

I look up at her, but she seems to be focused on something outside the window, one fist resting on her hip. I sign my name in the box and give her paper back.

"Where is your father?" I ask before my brain can stop me from being rude.

Still looking out the window, she answers, "Afghanistan." She turns and points her chin at my paper. "What about your dad?"

"At home. In Pakistan, I mean."

She frowns. "What's he doing there?"

I wish I knew, exactly. All I know is that my best friend's father and Baba are no longer friends, and Baba can't leave work until he finishes whatever it is that he needs to finish. But I can't say any of that, so instead I say, "He is waiting for his traveling visa." Because this is true, too. Before she can ask another question, I ask, "Why your father is in Afghanistan?"

"He's deployed."

I don't know that word, but whatever it means, she doesn't look very happy about it.

Jordan folds her arms. "He's in the army. Third time over there."

I don't know what to say to that. This is the first time I have been away from Baba, and it seems like forever ago since I saw him last. I cannot imagine having him back only to leave again, and again, and again.

Mrs. Wu calls us back to the carpet with our papers, and now we have to go around the circle and share one thing we learned about someone in the class.

"Who would like to go first?" Mrs. Wu asks.

I raise my hand. It is better to go now before someone takes my two answers.

"Bilal, what would you like to share?"

Jordan's head snaps up. I see her barely shake her head—

a movement so small I don't think anyone else notices. I nod once to tell her I won't talk about her father to anyone.

My eyes scan the kids in the circle until I find José's spiky black hair. I still don't know how to say his name, so I point to him and say, "He likes basketball."

Mrs. Wu nods. "Do you play on a team, José?"

So that's how you say his name—*ho-ZAY*.

Mrs. Wu thanks me and moves on. I learn from the others that Americans like pizza, hamburgers, and chicken nuggets. They like to vacation at places called the beach, Disney World, and Kings Dominion. I also learn that no one else's favorite subject is English; they say either science, social studies (I am not sure what this means), math, or something called *language arts*—maybe that is where we will do English and some other languages, along with art. Some people say their favorite subject is just art, without the *language* part. Lots of people say *PE*, and I don't know what that is, either. Everyone laughs when someone says recess, and I make a note in my brain to ask Jalaal about all of these things.

I start to tune out after a while because this much English hurts my head. The only thing these people know about me is that I have one sister and one brother. Jordan knows about Baba and baseball, of course. Which means the one person here I have something in common with is a girl. A girl my baseball friends want nothing to do with.

I miss Mudassar.

Thirteen

After the icebreaker, Mrs. Wu tells us to stand in a giant circle around the classroom. She stands in the circle with us, holding a foam ball as big as a melon.

"We're going to clear out our summer brains with a fun, easy math warm-up," she says, and everyone breaks into grins. I have never done math before with a ball, or standing up, or with everyone smiling. This will be a first.

Mrs. Wu opens her mouth to say something else, then stops and waves toward the door. A man with yellow hair and the beginnings of a beard stands in the doorway, his hand raised in a wave.

"Mr. Jacobs, come on in!"

He strides into the room with a clipboard. On his way over to Mrs. Wu, he gives one boy a high five. "Not coming with me this year, buddy!" Mr. Jacobs says.

The boy grins. "I passed my reading test," he says, and stands up straighter.

"I saw, man." Mr. Jacobs smiles. "With flying colors!"

Flying colors must be a good score, because Mr. Jacobs high-fives the boy once more.

Mrs. Wu gives the boy a thumbs-up. I imagine Mrs. Wu doing this gesture in front of my teachers in Pakistan, and I can't help it—a laugh escapes. I slap my hand over my mouth, and the boy with flying colors narrows his eyes. I want to tell him I am not laughing at him, but now everyone is looking at me, including the teachers.

Mrs. Wu waves me over. "Bilal, this is Mr. Jacobs, the ESL teacher. You'll be going with him for a bit this morning."

Mr. Jacobs shakes my hand. "Great to meet you, Bilal. What do you say? You ready?"

What I want to say is no, I am not ready to leave for ESL class. Not when we are about to play a math game.

But I have no choice. I follow Mr. Jacobs into the hall where three kids are waiting. None of us says a word as we head outside into the morning sun. I wonder if the others think it's weird that we are leaving the school building.

"Almost there, folks!" Mr. Jacobs says. We round a corner of the school and head up a ramp to another building—not big and brick like the school, but smaller and square and the color of sand. When we get to the door at the top of the ramp, Mr. Jacobs passes his badge over a gray box next to the door. There's a beep and a click, and the door unlocks. This must be a very important building if you need a badge to beep you in.

It doesn't look very important inside, though. It smells a little damp, and our footsteps make hollow sounds as we walk down the hall. We come to a door that reads Welcome! in about fifteen languages. I find the Urdu *Khush amdeed*, and it feels like it is there just for me.

Mr. Jacobs unlocks the door. "Come on in." He swings one arm wide, and we file in past him. A U-shaped table surrounded by dark blue plastic chairs takes up half the room. The sun streams in through a small window onto a neat stack of papers on Mr. Jacobs's desk.

Three of the walls are bare, but the fourth one is full of photos and posters—one says Istanbul, another Rome, and two are from somewhere in China. I scan the wall for a poster from Pakistan, but I don't see one.

"Take a look around, if you'd like."

No one moves at first, so Mr. Jacobs waves us over to the display of photos on the wall. Up close, I can see that Mr. Jacobs is in most of them—sometimes alone, and sometimes with other people. There's one of Mr. Jacobs on a camel in front of a pyramid, another of him standing on the steps of the Great Wall of China, and one where he is standing next to a pretty lady with long, dark hair who is holding a yellow-haired baby on a beach. He names the places in the photos, but there are no photos of Pakistan.

The girl standing next to me says she's from a place called Cartagena, Colombia. She seems excited about a photo of Mr. Jacobs standing on top of some fort overlooking the sea.

"Okay, everyone," Mr. Jacobs calls. "Let's take a seat."

We gather around the U-shaped table.

"You've seen my photos and heard a little bit about my travels. Now I'd love to hear about your first country."

"First country?" the boy next to me asks.

Mr. Jacobs nods. "Some people call the place where they come from their home country, but after a while, the United States might feel like home to you, too."

I don't say this to Mr. Jacobs, but I can't ever imagine feeling at home here.

"I grew up in lots of different places," Mr. Jacobs explains. "I didn't even live here in the United States until I was nine years old."

"Where you live?" someone asks.

"My parents were missionaries." He pauses and takes in our confused faces. "A missionary is someone who goes to another country to help people."

We nod, although I don't really understand. What kind of help?

"So we lived in China, Nepal, Tanzania, and Bolivia."

I try to imagine living so many places in nine years.

I raise my hand.

"Bilal, you don't have to raise your hand in here. With only four of you, we can take turns talking and still be respectful when it's someone else's turn."

I glance at the boy next to me, and he shrugs as if to say, "Look, I'm not used to this, either."

I ask, "You like moving all those times?"

Mr. Jacobs thinks about this before answering. "Not back then. But later I figured out that the hardest part of moving is right before you move. That's when you know what you'll be missing—friends, places—but you don't know yet what you'll be getting. You'll have friends in your new town; you just haven't met them yet."

I do not want to disagree with Mr. Jacobs, but for me, the

hardest part of moving is now. Or maybe the hardest part was saying good-bye to Baba. I decide they are two different kinds of hard that cannot be compared.

Mr. Jacobs taps a marker on the edge of the table. "Okay, now for introductions. We'll each say our name"—he uncaps the marker and writes something on a small whiteboard—"then where we're from, one thing we miss, and one thing we like about living here."

One girl speaks up for the first time. "What if nothing I like here?"

Mr. Jacobs adds something in parentheses to the whiteboard and holds it up for us to see:

1. My name is _____ .
2. I am from _____ .
3. One thing I miss from my first country is
    _____ .
4. One thing I like (or one thing that surprises me)
    about the USA is _____ .

He gives us a minute to read the board.

"Okay, I'll start," he says, pointing to the first sentence. "My name is Mr. Jacobs. I am from many places, but mostly Fairfax, Virginia. One thing I miss from Bolivia is playing soccer in the street. One thing I like about the United States is watching the Maryland Terps play basketball."

He pulls out a photo of a bunch of dark-haired kids and one yellow-haired boy playing soccer on a dusty road near some low houses made of stone. He passes it around, and I notice a date stamped on the back: December 1990. Next he shows us a magazine cover with a man wearing a tank top and shorts, slamming an orange ball into a basket. The words next to it read: Terps' Chance for Wild Card Slim to None.

"What do those words mean?" I ask, pointing to the magazine cover. It feels strange to blurt out a question without first raising my hand.

Mr. Jacobs slaps his hand onto his heart and sighs. "It means my team has not been winning the past few seasons. But they're still my favorite team."

In the next fifteen minutes, I learn that my ESL classmates are Sofia, Ana, and Samir. They come from El Salvador, Colombia, and Sudan. They miss things I have never heard of—*atole de elote*, *arroz con coco*, and *waika*. Sofia and Ana like pizza and frozen yogurt, and Samir is surprised by a kind of truck called *eighteen-wheeler*.

And then it's my turn.

I take a breath. "My name is Bilal. I am from Karachi, Pakistan." I check the whiteboard again so I won't make a mistake. "One thing I like about America is the air-conditioning."

Everyone laughs and nods.

"And what do you miss most, Bilal?" Mr. Jacobs asks.

It might seem like a hard question, because I miss so many things—too many to say in front of everyone. I miss my friends and my school. Knowing where to go in the city if I am hungry for an after-school snack like *makhai*, a cob of corn roasted over coals with red pepper and salt and wrapped in newspaper. I miss understanding everything people say, not just some things. And cricket. And searching for pebbles at Hawks Bay and seeing the green sea turtle babies hatch from their eggs and scuttle across the sand to the water.

But this question is actually an easy one, because of the word *most*.

I look at my hands, my voice quiet when I say, "The thing I miss most is my father."

Everyone is silent. I wonder if maybe I should have said a different answer—something funny or interesting. But then Mr. Jacobs asks, "Who else misses family in their first country?" All three of my classmates raise their hands, and I feel a little better. Not because I am happy they miss their families, but because I am not the only one.

When you feel alone, it is better to feel alone together.

✦　✦　✦

Lunch at this school is nothing like lunchtime at my old school. There is no food stand—there's a whole huge kitchen in the back with two counters long enough to fit ten kids across. There are plastic spoons instead of metal ones, and tiny cartons of milk instead of glass bottles of Coca-Cola poured into bags. Instead of paying in rupees, I have to punch in my lunch number on a keyboard. Luckily, Ammi made me memorize my number.

José sits next to me, although he spends his whole lunch talking to the boy sitting across from him. Jordan picks at her food down at the other end of the table, and it looks like her lunch is going about as well as mine is. The girls nearby talk around her like she's not even there. Then again, she doesn't seem to mind. She doesn't even try to talk to anyone. A girl with a dark brown braid down her back says something that makes the other girls drop their forks and lean in. Not Jordan—she just takes another bite of spaghetti, staring down at her pink foam tray.

Mrs. Wu strides into the cafeteria and heads for our table. "Are we ready?" She motions for us to stand, sending chair legs scraping against the tile floor. The class forms a line, and I follow the other kids to a side door.

"Yes! Recess time," José says.

Now I will finally discover what recess is.

The heat hits me like a wall when I step outside. I stop for a moment and squint in the bright sun. In Karachi it is hot—hotter than here, sometimes. But I'm not used to going from cool buildings into this heat.

Most kids race toward the playground or the grassy field. So recess must be Games Period. I scan the crowd, trying to find someone I recognize, but I don't spot anyone I know. All the kids run around, laughing and talking like they've known each other their whole lives.

"That's great you'll be training with the developmental team." Jordan's voice comes from right behind me.

She comes and stands next to me, arms folded.

"Thank you." I wonder why she thinks this is so great when she is the Cardinals' pitcher. Maybe she is making fun of me. But then she says, "Uncle Matt says this is your first time ever playing baseball. He told me you played some other sport back in Pakistan that's kind of like baseball."

I nod. "Cricket." I can tell by the look on her face that she does not know cricket. "We play with a bat and ball, but it is not so much like baseball."

She shrugs. "You're a good pitcher."

But not a good batter. Jordan doesn't say this, of course, but she must think it.

"Congratulations on being a Cardinal. You are happy, no?" I remember how she looked when no one clapped for her.

"Kind of." She kicks a pebble. "I mean, I love playing the game. But I can tell the other guys don't want me on their team."

I don't know what to say to that.

Jordan slips her hands into her pockets. "My dad taught me to play when I was little. He was my coach back in Illinois."

I smile. "My father was my cricket coach when I was little. He played on the national team."

Jordan raises an eyebrow. "Wow. He must be really good."

"Yes, a long time ago, but he never plays now. He hurt his knee."

Jordan nods. "A bum knee's the worst. Unless you're a pitcher." She grins. "If I could, I'd play in the majors for the American League when I grow up—the Chicago White Sox, if they'd take me. Then I wouldn't have to bat—I'd just pitch."

I didn't understand everything she said, but I did get the part about some pitchers not having to bat. I grin. "Maybe I will try out for these White Socks, then."

She frowns. "You'd probably make it, too."

"Not if you are trying out." I wish she would smile again.

"Only men get to play major-league baseball."

"Oh." I think for a minute. "In cricket, there is a world cup for women's teams, but it is not so popular like the men's world cup."

Jordan shrugs. "At least they have a world cup to play in."

"No women's teams are in the baseball world cup?"

Her smile is back. "It's called the World Series. And no,

there isn't one for women. There used to be, back in the old days, but not anymore."

A red ball rolls our way from the blacktop, and Jordan gives it a strong kick back.

"What about the Olympics?" I offer.

She shakes her head. "No baseball in the Olympics, period. Not even for men anymore."

"No cricket, either," I say.

We stand there in silence for a few seconds. There are a lot of reasons not to play a sport—no talent, no money, no good fields for games. But I never thought about not playing just because you're a girl.

I wonder out loud: "How much longer can you play on a baseball team?"

Jordan sighs. "Through high school. That's pretty much it."

I remember what Akash said about softball and ask Jordan if she could play that.

"Nah. The pitching is totally different. Baseball's better."

It seems like if she likes baseball best, she should be able to play it as long as she wants. "Maybe they can change the rules or something?"

Jordan shrugs. "Maybe." But she does not look convinced.

Another class flows out from the side door onto the playground.

"Bilal!" Henry breaks off from the crowd and holds up a big, orange ball. "Let's shoot some hoops!"

I look at Jordan and lower my voice. "I am not sure what that means."

She shades her eyes with her hand and looks over at Henry. "Basketball. He's asking you to play."

Now Akash has joined Henry and is waving me over, too.

I wonder if Jordan plays this game of basketball. When I take a breath to ask, she cuts me off. "Go ahead. They'll show you what to do."

I spot Mr. Jacobs out there, too, and take two steps away from Jordan. Then I turn. "I see you later, okay?"

Jordan nods.

I join the guys and do not look back. If I do, I might change my mind.

"You're not hanging out with her, are you?" Henry looks at me warily.

"She is in my class."

Akash sighs. "Man, bad luck. Hopefully you don't have to sit next to her."

I don't tell them that we already sit in the same group. I also don't tell them that I am glad to know at least one person in my class, even if that one person is a girl.

We reach the blacktop, where Mr. Jacobs stands under one of the baskets. He raises his hand in a wave. "Hey, Bilal! You and your friends up for a game?"

My friends. It feels good to have friends.

We join the game, and it only takes about three minutes for me—and everyone else—to discover that basketball is yet another American sport I am not good at.

Mercifully, Mrs. Wu finally blows a whistle and holds up her hand, sending kids running into line. Jordan stands a few kids behind me. Her hands are shoved into her pockets, and the toe of her shoe digs a hole in the dirt as we wait for the last of the stragglers to join the line.

I feel worse for Jordan than ever. I should ask her to play

basketball with us next time. Maybe Akash and Henry would get to know her and be her friend, too.

But then I think of the way they acted when they saw me standing next to her.

When our line starts moving, I turn away from Jordan and follow everyone else back inside.

# Fourteen

September passes, and still no Baba. The Cardinals practice three afternoons a week, and our developmental team practices on the field next to theirs. We aren't a team really. We don't play real games, we don't have uniforms, and we don't even have a real name. Henry decides to fix the name problem, and we vote on the phoenix as our mascot.

"It's a bird, but better than a cardinal," Henry says.

Apparently it is a mythical bird that rose from some ashes. Coach Matt calls that a metaphor for our team, which I don't really understand.

No matter what we are called, it is painfully obvious that we Phoenixes are not ready to be Cardinals.

Akash told me how to figure out my batting average, and it's .120. I think this is a big improvement, considering my average used to be .000. But it's still not good enough for the Cardinals.

The one good thing about practicing next to the Cardinals is that I can study Jordan's pitches and try to figure out how she strikes out so many players. Sometimes she pretends not to be ready, then she lets the ball fly. Other times she actually yawns and you think she's getting tired or bored, but then the ball is suddenly in Akash's catcher's mitt and you don't even know how it happened.

The best part of practices is definitely the pitching clinics, when it's just me, Coach Pablo, and Jordan. Coach Pablo teaches us how to be better pitchers, while the other kids learn how to be better catchers or shortstops or whatever position they play. During pitching clinics, everyone knows I have to work with Jordan, so no one suspects that sometimes we talk about non-baseball things like our fathers and our homes before we came here.

But I have to stay focused and work harder to become a great pitcher like Jordan. I have to practice batting and catching with a glove. I have to move up and play with the Cardinals so Baba will keep his promise to get here in time to see me play in a real game.

"Okay, folks!" Coach Matt calls. "Time for some conditioning." There's a groan that sounds a lot like Jack, and Coach Matt folds his arms. "Anyone who doesn't like that can go home."

Silence.

"All right, ten laps around the bases clockwise, then ten more counterclockwise." He pauses, as if he's daring Jack to moan again. When no one makes a sound, he continues. "Then we'll break up into our groups according to position, followed by batting practice, then a scrimmage." He nods toward our bags. "I hope everyone brought water. This Indian summer's been a doozy. Isn't this supposed to be October?" He glances at Coach Pablo, who shakes his head.

I don't know what a doozy is, but it is true that summers in India are very hot.

We start our twenty runs around the bases. Trees as tall as our apartment building back home ring the field, and the colors of the leaves blur together as I run—green, red, yellow, orange, and brown. Fall leaves are the latest addition to my American list of things for Baba to know. I even sent him pictures that show how some leaves have more than one color. But you can't take a picture of the way they smell or feel when you wade through them, crunching and kicking and jumping. Baba's latest Karachi memory for me was pistachio Peshawari ice cream, which only reminds me that while I'm jumping in piles of leaves, my friends back home still jump in the warm sea.

Coach Matt looks at his watch as we finish our baserunning. He nods. "Not bad."

We take it as a compliment. His phone sounds from his pocket, a song I now know is "Sweet Caroline" and has something to do with the Boston Red Sox—Coach Matt's favorite team. Coach Pablo shakes his head and covers his ears. I have learned that Coach Pablo is a Yankees fan, and Yankees fans don't like this song.

We break into our clinic groups, and I am paired with Jordan. Coach Matt slides his phone into his back pocket. "Got a minute, Pablo?"

Coach Pablo turns to Jordan and me. "You two start warming up. I'll be right there." He turns back to Coach Matt, and they talk about the tournament the Cardinals will play in this weekend.

Jordan points her glove toward a grassy strip well beyond second base. "Let's go."

We head over, listening to the sounds of our cleats swooshing through the grass, the crack of a bat meeting a ball, and players' voices floating across the field.

Jordan breaks the sounds of baseball with this question: "So when is your dad getting here?"

I slow my steps, and Jordan falls back to match my pace.

"I don't know. He always says 'soon,' but . . ."

And I leave it at that.

Jordan sighs. "It's never soon enough. I know."

"How long is your father in Afghanistan?"

The muscle in her jaw tightens. "Three months so far. He spent a whole year there before—two different times."

"When will he come home?"

Jordan picks up her pace, her eyes on the cars that snake along the road beyond the field. "Next summer."

I start to ask why she is here and not in the place called Illinois, but she breaks into a jog. "You can pitch first, okay?" she calls over her shoulder. I stop where I am and wait for her to turn. She finally does, slipping on the catcher's mask and punching her glove three times before crouching and turning her glove out. "Ready?" she calls.

I nod, lift my right knee, and send a slow pitch. She catches it easily, stands, and throws it back, all in a series of fluid movements. She almost looks bored. When I get to my last pitch, a fast one, I draw in a breath. I know her fastest pitches are faster than mine, but I want to make this a good one. I don't know why, but I want to show her I'm getting better.

I raise my right knee like always and pull my left arm back

114

as my right arm stretches forward, keeping my balance. I stay like that for a few moments, and Jordan's bored expression is replaced by another one—curiosity. Before she can wonder another second longer, I let the ball fly, hurling it through the thick, mid-October air. Jordan catches it easily, but she shakes her head as she studies the ball in her glove.

Then she stands and nods once. "Okay, my turn."

I pull on the catcher's mask and get into position, but I slip off my glove for the first slow pitches. After she sends her medium pitch, my hand stings. I want to shake it out and flex my fingers, but I don't. I do slip my glove on for the fast pitch, though. Even if I can't catch as well with it on, I'm not stupid.

Jordan nods. I nod back and send up a small prayer to Allah that this ball will miss my knee and my shoulder and my head and find its way into my glove.

It does. I don't even need to move my glove; it's like the ball decided it was meant to be there.

As I stand to stretch my legs, Coach Pablo jogs over. "Sorry about the delay."

I toss him the ball. "No problem, Coach."

"I just saw some excellent pitching." He nods at Jordan, then turns to me. "Nice job catching, Bilal."

I wonder if he knows I wasn't really catching; I was just holding the glove in the right place at the right time.

We work for another half hour with Coach Pablo before Coach Matt calls us over for a practice scrimmage.

As we get closer to the dugout, I spot Henry whispering something to Aiden. They laugh.

I turn to Jordan. "Um, I need some water." Before she can answer, I am jogging toward the dugout. When I get there, I dig through my bag, pull out my water bottle, and join the rest of the team. I don't stand anywhere near Jordan.

Coach Matt pats the shoulder of a boy I've never seen before, then calls, "All right, folks, quiet down." He turns to the boy. "This is Sebastian. He and his family just moved to DC, and he's looking to join a team."

Sebastian waves. "Hey," he says, and we say "hey" back.

"I heard he's also trying out for some powerhouse team up in Maryland," Akash whispers. "Or maybe he'll end up being a Cardinal."

I shrug. I just hope he's not a pitcher.

The scrimmage begins and Jordan is on a roll, as Jalaal would say. We get two outs—one when Jack strikes out, and one when Nate's ball is caught in the outfield.

Sebastian is up next, and I pray he gets out so I can start pitching instead of worrying about batting. Sebastian saunters over to home plate like he's got all the time in the world. Jordan wears her usual calm expression; she doesn't seem nervous at all about pitching to someone new.

Sebastian taps the base once with his bat, then moves around to the other side of the base. He lifts his bat, ready to go.

He is a lefty, like me.

Jordan's mask of calm indifference slips for a moment while she adjusts her stance. Before she pulls her arm back, she bites the corner of her lip, and I can tell she isn't sure about this Sebastian. She fires off a fastball—faster than any ball she's ever sent my way.

Sebastian may be a southpaw like me, but unlike me, he can hit. He sends Jordan's fastball over everyone's head, where no infielder can reach it. The outfielders scramble below the ball's path as it traces an arc before falling back to earth in an empty patch of field. By the time someone snatches it up, Sebastian is already rounding third base and heading home. His foot lands on home plate in a spectacular cloud of dirt. No one even tried to throw the ball to Akash, and he takes off his catcher's mask, shaking his head.

Jordan has her hands on her hips, her eyes narrowed under the shadow of her cap.

I'm up next. Even though Jordan strikes me out as usual, I can tell it doesn't make her feel any better.

We practice until the sun sets and the lights go on, the sky a glowing orange that fades to purple.

I walk to the dugout to get my bag.

Henry points his chin in Jordan's direction as she marches off toward the parking lot. "Did you guys see what happened out there?"

Akash's eyes grow wide. "Man, she totally choked!"

Henry's laugh is mean. "It finally took a lefty to show her she's not perfect."

I don't mention that I'm a lefty and she strikes me out all the time.

Henry smirks. "What a show-off."

I start to say that Jordan isn't showing off—she really is that good. But then Henry gives me a friendship shoulder-punch and says, "You could outpitch her any day."

I give him a friendship shoulder-punch back. And leave it at that.

 # Fifteen

"What are you going to be for Halloween?" Jalaal rummages through his drawer for clean socks. He doesn't find any.

I sit on my bed, passing a baseball from one hand to the other. "I have my cricket uniform. But I cannot wear that."

"Why not?" Jalaal asks, holding his hand out for the ball. I toss it to him, and he sends it back.

"We have to dress like a book character for the school Halloween parade and carry the book with us." I throw the ball back a little too hard, and Jalaal has to lean into the catch.

"I remember doing that. It's crazy that you can't just wear whatever you want." He strides over to his bookshelf and runs a finger over the book spines. He shakes his head. "I can't think of one story about a cricket-playing kid."

I picture my bookshelf back home and wish I'd brought one of my cricket books.

Jalaal's phone beeps. He glances at it and grins. "I've got an idea."

Ten minutes later we walk into the public library. I thought public libraries were for scholars and studying and grown-ups. Not this one. Big, orange vegetables that Jalaal calls pumpkins sit on a table surrounded by fake spiders, a web, and books with mostly orange or black covers. A banner hanging from the ceiling says, "Scare up a good book!" A gray, rock-looking piece of foam with a rounded top reads:

R.I.P.
Read in Peace

Jalaal heads straight for a computer. He types and clicks. "Cricket . . . there has to be something here."

"How about a book about Omar Khan?" I offer.

Jalaal shakes his head. "Nothing." He keeps typing.

How can a library not have a book about the world's greatest cricket player?

"There's one!" Jalaal looks triumphant. "Seven ninety-six point three five eight."

"What?" I ask.

"This way," he says, repeating the number under his breath.

I follow him past babies chewing on books and tables of grown-ups and kids reading and doing homework. Jalaal glances at the signs at the end of each shelf until he stops, turns, and pulls a book from up high.

"This is the only one I could find." He hands me a book called *Learn to Play Cricket* with a photo of a cricket ball on the cover.

"Thank you, Jalaal." I flip through the pages and smile. This is stuff I know, but it is perfect for the Halloween parade.

"No problem, little buddy."

Jalaal's phone beeps again, and his texting thumbs fly over the screen. When he looks up, a grin spreads across his face. I follow his gaze to where Olivia sits at a table with a stack of books. She waves us over, but before I take a step, Jalaal puts his hand on my shoulder. "Hey, Bilal, why don't you see if there are any other books you might like? I'll meet you back here in five minutes."

I get it—I'm not a little kid anymore. I can tell Jalaal likes Olivia, and I can also tell Auntie doesn't want Jalaal to have a girlfriend. I heard them arguing one time when Auntie said Jalaal is too young, and Jalaal said he is not too young to have a girl for a friend. Being seventeen sounds complicated.

As promised, Jalaal meets me back in the same spot five minutes later. We check out the cricket book, and Jalaal gets me my own library card. I sign the back, slip it into my pocket, and smile all the way out to the car.

I flip through the pages of *Learn to Play Cricket*. It will feel good to wear my uniform again, even if it's not for a match. I can't wait for Halloween.

✦   ✦   ✦

On Monday everyone boards the bus clutching their Halloween costume bags. Most people are keeping their costumes a secret, but Akash tells me he's going as Harry Potter. I peek at the white cricket uniform in my trash bag. Maybe I should have dressed like Harry Potter, too. I've read all the books in Urdu, and people would at least know who I am.

During morning meeting, Mrs. Wu holds her own bag on

120

her lap—a huge, black trash bag. Whatever's inside is long and has lumps. "Okay, a few reminders about today." She smiles. "I know it's Halloween, and you've all got candy on the brain."

Everyone laughs, and it feels good to understand her joke.

"But before the parade this afternoon, we still need to focus on things like math, science, language arts, and social studies."

Tristan shudders. "Scary," he says, and even Mrs. Wu laughs.

"Instead of our usual morning greeting, I want everyone to think of one clue about your costume or about the book it's related to. I'll begin."

Mrs. Wu pulls her bag closer and props her elbows on top. "My favorite book"—Mrs. Wu pats the bag with a solid thump—"showed me that sometimes the things we run away from are the very things we need most."

I am relieved to see that the other kids look as confused as I am.

"Okay, who would like to go next?"

I think of what I'll say about my book—one I've never read—as the others give their clues.

"This is *some* book!"

"Mine's a diary—maybe dorky, maybe wimpy. You'll find out at the parade."

"The title of my favorite book could be worn as a necklace."

"You won't guess mine unless you follow the rules."

"Mine is super hard to guess."

With each clue some people look confused and others look thoughtful; I look confused for each and every one. My turn is next, and I am clueless. This means I do not have a clue about what clue to give.

"Bilal?" Mrs. Wu smiles, and nods at my bag.

I swallow. "My book . . . ," I begin, and then stop. My book, what? Is a book I've never read? Is full of information I already know? I glance at Jordan, who's got a look on her face that says, "Well? What is it?"

Then I have an idea. "My book is not about a bug."

Mrs. Wu waits, like she's thinking that maybe I'll say more, but I don't. That's my clue. I'm no longer clueless.

I don't listen to the next clues, because I know I won't know these books. I should ask Mr. Jacobs how I can hurry up and learn enough English to read the same books everyone else can read.

I do pay attention when it's Jordan's turn. She holds up a brown paper lunch bag, and I wonder what kind of costume could fit inside a bag so small. She looks down, running her fingers along the creased top of the bag. Then she looks up and says, "Yes, and . . ."

And that's it.

Everyone looks confused except for Mrs. Wu, who says, "I'm glad you're enjoying that one, Jordan."

Jordan nods without looking up from her bag.

The rest of the morning flies by. The best part of the day is when we open real pumpkins for math. We work in groups of four, estimating weight, circumference, and the number of seeds inside the pumpkin. I say our pumpkin must weigh about five hundred grams, but no one in my group seems to know what that means. As it turns out, our pumpkin weighs fifteen ounces, and I don't understand what that means. But Mrs. Wu says I'll come in handy when we talk about the metric system. Coming in handy sounds like a nice thing to be.

Finally we change into our costumes and gather in a circle around our desks. Kids hold up their books, and people say things like, "Oh! *Charlotte's Web!*" and "*Dork Diaries*—I knew it!" and "*Amulet!*" and "I love *Rules!*" I don't know any of these books. Well, okay, except for Lucas's book about some super-heroes that I've seen before on TV.

José looks at my V-necked sweater vest. He points to the small crest and says, "What are you supposed to be—a kid at some private school?"

Before I can answer, Mrs. Wu holds up her hand for quiet.

Mrs. Wu has changed into a denim dress with tights and sneakers and a jacket. She's holding a violin case and a book with a cover that reads *From the Mixed-Up Files of Mrs. Basil E. Frankweiler.* I don't even understand what the title means, so this book is probably too hard for me anyway. She explains she is dressed like the main character in the story, some girl named Claudia who runs away from home and goes to live in a museum, all because her parents don't appreciate her. It sounds like maybe Claudia missed her parents even though they all lived in the same house in the same city in the same country.

Jordan is dressed in normal clothes—jeans and a T-shirt with a picture of a yellow bow across the front. She spins a roll of masking tape around her wrist like a bracelet. For her turn, she says, "Mrs. Wu recommended this book. It's called *Operation Yes* by Sara Lewis Holmes, and it's about kids on a military base who are waiting for their parents to come back from being deployed." Jordan holds up her wrist to show the masking tape. "Their teacher is Miss Loupe, who tapes a space on the floor, and the kids have to improvise different situations. When they think up one thing, Miss Loupe always says, 'Yes, and . . . ,' and they have to keep adding on ideas."

I guess that explains why Jordan's clue this morning was "Yes, and . . . ," but I still have no idea what Jordan's book is about. What does *improvise* mean? Why would a teacher put tape on the floor?

My head hurts thinking of all these books I can't read yet. And then it's my turn.

I hold up *Learn to Play Cricket*.

Everyone is silent as they peer at the cover and then at my uniform.

I clear my throat. "My clue was that my book is not about a bug."

Mrs. Wu nods. "That was a good clue, Bilal."

"So what are you, then?" Teah asks.

I point to my book's cover. "This."

Half the class laughs, and I remember now that my book's cover does not have a picture of a player, just a ball.

"Ladies and gentlemen." Mrs. Wu's voice carries a warning.

I swallow. "In Pakistan I play cricket."

Mrs. Wu smiles. "And that handsome uniform must be your team uniform."

There are no snickers this time, but I can tell Jackson wants to laugh by the way he's gnawing on his lip. I wish Mrs. Wu hadn't said "handsome."

"Yes, this is my team uniform. But in America now I play baseball."

Dylan raises his hand but doesn't wait for Mrs. Wu to call on him. "How do you play cricket?"

"It has many rules," I say, because where would I even

begin? I hold up my book. "You can read to know the rules." I smile.

Dylan shrugs like he has already decided he is not going to learn about cricket.

Someone else says, "Man, those are some tall shin guards." No one laughs, but I see the nudges and grins and whispering lips. I look at my leg guards sticking up past my knees. Tall? Tall compared to what? We don't wear shin guards in baseball, so I don't know what other kind there is. I'm already outgrowing these pads from last year, so I'll need a bigger size this season. Or I would have, if we'd stayed in Pakistan.

Madi raises her hand. "I've seen cricket." She holds up her book, called *Doctor Who: Character Encyclopedia*. "I saw it on *Doctor Who* this one time."

A few kids nod, like Madi's statement now proves cricket really is a game and not something I made up.

The rest of the kids say what their costumes are, but I'm not listening. I'm wishing I could change out of this uniform that everyone thinks is weird. The parade isn't much better. Everyone in the entire school sits outside on the grass. Classes take turns parading around in a circle so everyone can see their books and their costumes. When our class's turn comes, kids peer at my book, trying to figure out what I am. The only person who doesn't look at me like I'm some alien is Mr. Jacobs. He gives me a high five as I walk by and says, "Cricket, huh? Nice, Bilal!"

But it's not nice—it's different.

The worst part is there's no time to change before the buses arrive, so I have to ride home in my uniform. Why does it have to be white and so bright? I don't know if people are still staring at me or not, because I lean my head against the window and watch the houses stream by all the way to my stop.

When I get off the bus, Jordan is waiting for me on the sidewalk.

"I like your costume." She falls into step beside me.

"Thank you." I glance over to see if she's making fun of me.

She shrugs. "It's unique. No one else had on a cricket uniform."

"I know." I sigh. "Only me."

"That's what makes it cool."

She is not making fun of me after all. I always thought Jordan hated being the only girl on our baseball team, but maybe she doesn't mind being different; maybe *different* is just a part of who she is.

I still don't know what her costume is supposed to be, so I make a guess. "Are you a present?"

Jordan looks at me funny. "A present?"

I point to the roll of masking tape around her wrist. "The tape is maybe for the wrapping paper? And the bow on your T-shirt?"

She grins. "The tape is something the characters use in the book—they act things out in this space that their teacher tapes on the floor."

I nod; Jordan already said this in class. But I still do not understand.

Jordan points to her shirt. "People tie yellow ribbons around trees when they're waiting for a solider they love to come home."

When we reach Jordan's house, now I understand why the tree trunk in her front yard is circled with a wide yellow ribbon.

She shrugs her backpack off her shoulder. "Maybe I'll see you around tonight trick-or-treating."

And with that, she heads inside.

Once I get home, I hang up my cricket uniform in the back of my closet. Since the Phoenixes don't have real uniforms, Jalaal digs through a basement box and finds a musty-smelling Cardinals uniform that he wore when he was ten.

Trick-or-treating is not as fun as I thought it would be. Akash and Henry invited me to go with them, but when Ammi and Auntie insisted they go with us, I told the guys to go on ahead. Yes, I am getting a lot of free candy. But I am the only fifth grader who is stuck trick-or-treating with his little sister. Other kids from my grade race together from house to house, their parents trailing a few houses behind. Kids my age don't actually go *with* their parents.

But Ammi and Auntie don't seem to understand how trick-or-treating works for big kids. They come with us to every door, pushing the stroller with Humza dressed like a pumpkin. They insist on taking pictures next to the decorations outside every house.

"I don't need to be in all the pictures, Ammi."

Hira tugs at my hand. "Yes! You do!"

Auntie laughs. "We'll send them to your father, and to Daddo, too—she'll want to see you all dressed up!"

I try not to roll my eyes as I stand behind Hira. Again. Humza decides he wants to walk, so we have to slow our steps while he waddles down the sidewalk, pushing his stroller.

By now I am wishing I had stayed home with Jalaal and Uncle to hand out candy.

Jordan's house is one of our last stops. This is really Coach

Matt's house, so I expect him to answer. Instead, Jordan's mom opens the door.

"Trick-or-treat!" Hira shrieks, holding out her bulging sack.

Jordan's mom laughs and tucks her hair behind one ear. "What a beautiful fairy!" She drops candy into Hira's bag.

"I am a fairy *princess*," Hira clarifies.

Jordan's mom nods knowingly. "Of course you are. You look beautiful."

Hira giggles a thank-you and then turns back to me. "Bilal! Come and get some candy!"

So much for pretending I am not with the fairy princess.

Hira scurries down the front step, practically running me over as I approach the door. I hold out my bag, and Jordan's mom leans forward, peering at my baseball uniform. She smiles and stands up straight. "You play for the Cardinals!" Turning, she calls, "Jordan! Another one of your teammates is here. Come and say hello!"

Jordan's face appears from around the door, and she breaks into a grin when she sees me. "Hey, Bilal." She steps out into the porch light.

When she sees my costume, her smile fades. She stands with her hands on her hips. "Where's your cricket uniform?"

I feel like an imposter wearing a Cardinals uniform, even if it is seven years old. I hold up my baseball glove like that explains everything. "It belongs to Jalaal."

She peers at the trick-or-treat bag threaded through my bat. "Yeah, but the cricket uniform is different. You're the only one who has one."

"Exactly." Why does she look so disappointed? Why does she even care what my costume is?

Hira tugs at my shirt. "Come on, Bilal!"

I step down off the porch. "I will see you tomorrow."

Jordan nods. "See you." And she shuts the door.

I didn't do anything wrong. So why do I feel so guilty?

# Sixteen

The end of the fall baseball season is here, and Baba is not. He missed the whole thing. Or maybe he didn't miss anything at all, since I didn't play in a single game.

Today is our team end-of-season party at the Slice of Heaven Pizzeria, with all the Cardinals and the Phoenixes. When Ammi and I walk in, the smell of the pizza brings me back to cricket team pizza parties in Karachi, which makes me miss Baba even more. Lots of other teams are here, including a soccer team with one girl I recognize from school.

Akash waves. "Bilal! Over here!"

Ammi fiddles with her *dupatta*, weaving the ends of the scarf through her fingers. She smiles. "Go on, Bilal. Join your friends."

It hits me that this is the first time Ammi has been anywhere in America without Auntie or Uncle. Ammi is learning English, but she doesn't speak it very often.

Henry waves me over to where he stands with Akash and some other kids.

"Hey, Bilal." Akash leans in, lowering his voice. "We're talking about who's gonna get MVP."

"MVP?"

"Most valuable player," they say in unison, then look around to see if anyone heard them.

I tune out of their conversation when I look over at Ammi, standing alone and still fingering the ends of her scarf. She moves toward the end of the table and pats a folded napkin, with a fork and knife nested inside, like it's the most interesting object in the world.

Behind Ammi, Jordan walks into the room with her mom. Jordan sees me, then looks away. I don't think she'll come over as long as I'm standing with the guys, so maybe I should go and say hello. I wonder if I could slip away without the guys noticing.

Before I can decide what to do, Coach Matt raises a hand. "Okay, folks!"

We all quiet down.

"First of all, welcome to our end-of-season gathering."

Coach Pablo nods toward the parents. "Please have a seat." He waves his hand to the left end of the table and says, "Parents at this end of the table." Then he waves his hand to the right. "And players at this end."

All the guys scramble to take a seat, but I am torn. Akash waves me over to a chair next to him, but I keep glancing over at Ammi. She stands back as parents fill in the seats at their half of the table, chatting and laughing with one another. Ammi chooses a chair at the end of the parents' section near the middle of the table. She exchanges a smile with the lady across from her, but then the lady continues her conversation with someone else. Ammi leans her arm on the back of the empty chair next to her. She looks so alone. I am not the only one who wishes Baba were here.

"Bilal—come on." Henry jabs his finger at the open seat across from him, the spot next to Akash. I take two steps in that direction, then stop.

"Hold on," I say. "I need to ask my mom something."

I slip into the seat next to Ammi, and she looks surprised.

"Bilal, is everything okay?" Ammi frowns and puts her hand over mine. I slip my hand out from under hers, hoping none of the guys saw that.

"I'm fine, Ammi. I just thought I'd sit over here."

Ammi's face softens. "Bilal, go sit with your friends. Have fun!" She smoothes her paper placemat.

Henry slides into the seat next to me and waves Akash over, just as Jordan and her mom come to stand behind the seats across from us. "Are these taken?" Jordan's mom asks.

"Please." Ammi nods and points an open hand at the chairs. "For you."

Jordan's mom smiles and tucks a strip of blonde hair behind her ear. "Thank you."

Henry doesn't look happy to see Jordan sitting across from us, but he doesn't say anything.

"See?" I whisper to Ammi in Urdu. "Now I am sitting with friends."

This seems to satisfy Ammi. She smiles and, thankfully, does not try to pat my hand again.

"Pizza!" someone calls.

"Careful—they're hot!" a waitress says, placing a raised tray of pizza between Jordan and me. "We've got eight pizzas here to start, with more coming out." She points at the first pizza at the adults' end of the table. "The first pizza is cheese, then pepperoni, next one's Hawaiian, then sausage." Now she points to the other far end of the table. "Same lineup here—we've got cheese first"—her hand follows the pizza path toward the middle of the table—"then pepperoni, Hawaiian, and sausage."

I was hoping one would be a *mirch masala* pizza, the kind I always used to get. Henry loads up his plate with pepperoni pizza slices, and Akash gets two slices of Hawaiian. Akash takes a bite of the pineapple-and-ham pizza and closes his eyes. "Bilal, you've gotta taste this."

I scan all the pizzas. "I can't have any with meat. Cheese pizza is fine for me."

Henry stops, mid-chew. "Why can't you have meat?"

I've never had to explain *halal* to anyone before. Ammi pauses, setting her fork on the edge of her plate. "Go on," she whispers in Urdu. "I'll help you explain if you need me to."

Now everyone is watching and waiting for my answer.

"Muslims only eat meat that is *halal*." I can tell by their faces that my words have not explained anything. "*Halal* means what we are allowed to eat. We can only eat meat from animals that are killed in a very quick way so the animals suffer not so much."

One mother puts down her slice of pepperoni pizza and looks at it like she's not hungry anymore.

Shortstop Ben says, "Sounds kind of like *kosher*."

Akash adds, "We don't eat beef at our house."

Jordan shakes her head. "I make it a point to always avoid eggplant."

Second baseman Carlos grabs another piece of pizza. "And I don't eat any green vegetables."

Carlos's mother wags a fork in her son's direction. "I heard that, Carlos Riccardo Vasquez de la Fuente," she says, and we all laugh.

Everyone goes back to eating, and Ammi gives me a smile. "Well done, Bilal."

I look at the guys and Jordan. All of us are actually talking and laughing our way through the rest of our pizza, without worrying about baseball. For the first time, it feels like maybe all of us could be friends.

"Ladies and gentlemen!" Coach Pablo stands near a small table filled with trophies and two medals.

Coach Matt joins him. "Hope you all enjoyed the pizza!"

Everyone cheers, including the parents. Even Ammi smiles and calls out, "Very good!"

Coach Pablo puts on tiny reading glasses that I have never seen him wear and unfolds a piece of paper. He clears his throat. "It has been our distinct honor to work with your sons, and daughter"—he smiles at Jordan—"this season."

Scattered laughter ripples through the room, and Jordan's cheeks turn a pepperoni color.

Coach Matt nods. "Every one of you has worked your tail off this season, and it shows. The Cardinals had the winning-est record this fall since I've been coaching, and the developmental team—our Phoenixes—came a long, long way."

Coach Pablo picks up a trophy. "Okay, players, when I call your name, come on up and claim your well-earned trophy."

When they get to my name, Ammi's eyes shine and she claps the loudest. Once everyone has a trophy, two medals remain.

Coach Matt holds up a thick blue ribbon, a medal dangling from the end that glints as it catches the light. "This is the award for the most improved player of the season."

Murmurs race around the table. For a second I wonder if it could be me, but I don't think I have improved all that much. Henry has gotten a lot better, and he's hoping the coaches will move him up to the Cardinals for the spring season. Everyone has improved, though, so I'm not sure who it will be.

Coach Matt waves everyone down to quiet. "I don't think this will be a big surprise for anyone." He nods. "This award is going to a player who, before July, had never even touched a baseball or a bat in his life."

Everyone swivels around and grins at me. My heart fills all the way to the top as I take a shaky breath. Coach Matt gives me a thumbs-up and I give him one back. "This player continues to show up at every practice, at every scrimmage, and gives his best. If he keeps going at this rate, he'll be unstoppable. Let's hear it for our very own southpaw . . . Bilal!"

The room erupts into applause, and my legs feel wobbly as I make my way to the awards table. Coach Matt shakes my hand, and I bow my head as he puts the medal around my neck.

Coach Pablo motions for everyone to quiet down. With his hand on my shoulder, he says one more thing. "We'd like to invite Bilal to play with the Cardinals in the spring."

I am a Cardinal?

I am a Cardinal!

Everyone is on their feet, clapping and hollering just for me. I think of how loudly Daddo would cheer if she were here. Ammi's eyes brim with tears. I look away from the pride on her face because I know she is thinking what I am thinking, that the only thing that would make this day better is to have Baba here.

As I make my way back to my seat, everyone's hands are out for high fives, and I slap each one until I reach Ammi, who pulls me into a hug.

Jordan offers her high five over the table. "Way to go, Bilal!" Her grin is contagious, and my cheeks hurt from smiling.

It's a good thing that other lefty, Sebastian, picked some Maryland team over the Cardinals, or I might still be a Phoenix.

Coach Pablo picks up the next medal, and everyone quiets down. "This next one is for our MVP—most valuable player."

The guys all lean forward in their chairs a centimeter or two. The Cardinals did so well this fall, and there are lots of players who could get this one.

Coach Pablo holds up the medal. "Although this award is called the Most Valuable Player, we want you to know we value each and every one of you."

Coach Matt nods.

"That said, there is one player who stands out." Coach Pablo takes a breath. "This player consistently performs well, consistently works hard, and consistently makes a difference on the scoreboard in each and every game." He smiles. "Please join me in congratulating . . . Jordan!"

Jordan gasps. But instead of looking overjoyed, the color has drained from her face. Everyone claps and some even cheer, but the celebration is nothing compared to mine. No one stands.

Jordan's mom throws her arms around her. "Oh, honey. I'm so proud. Your dad will be so proud!"

Jordan makes her way to the awards table. The clapping continues, and when she turns, her mom stands. I stand, too, and so do the parents. The rest of the team stands, one by one, but there is no whooping or hollering this time.

When she gets back to the table, I high-five Jordan, but Henry and the other guys don't.

Coach Matt calls, "Who's up for dessert?"

Waiters bring out bowls of vanilla ice cream and smaller bowls with sprinkles and toppings. I think about taking my medal off so I won't spill ice cream on the ribbon, but I decide to leave it on and just be very, very careful. I can't wait to tell Baba about winning, and maybe I'll even bring my medal to ESL class to show Mr. Jacobs. I wish I could tell Mudassar.

I bet Jordan's dad will be proud that she won MVP. When I open my mouth to ask when she'll get to talk to him next, she slips her medal from around her neck. She wraps the ribbon around it and stuffs the whole thing in her pocket.

Henry leans over and whispers to me: "Even Jordan knows she doesn't deserve MVP."

When Henry was a guest player for one of the Cardinals' games, his dad spent most of the time yelling at the umpire, asking if he was blind. I should ask Henry the same thing. I should ask him if he's ever seen Jordan pitch, because she definitely deserves that medal.

But I don't.

Henry goes back to his ice cream and to whatever he was talking about before with the guys.

I try to catch Jordan's eye to figure out if she heard Henry's words, but she doesn't look up. She stirs her ice cream until the sprinkles disappear.

Seventeen

When I wake up on Thanksgiving morning, I don't open my eyes right away. My family's voices drift up the stairs and into my room. Uncle says something I can't quite make out, followed by laughter. The sound of Hira's and Humza's bare feet slapping against the wood floor mixes with squeals and giggles.

"Stop, Jalaal!" they plead, with voices that make it clear they don't want Jalaal to stop tickling them or chasing them or whatever he's doing to make them laugh.

Auntie calls, "Jalaal, stop tormenting the children!" but her warning dissolves into laughter.

I try to imagine Baba's laughter mixed in with the others, but I can't do it. It feels like forever since I've heard his voice. Luckily today we don't have school, so he is going to call us after he gets home from work. I've got so much to tell him, like why today is a holiday. Mrs. Wu said that a long time ago,

138

some people from England were saved by people from America, and they had a big feast to say thank you. The people who did the thanking were called Pilgrims, and the people who did the saving were called all kinds of things. Jack calls them Indians, but Akash says they aren't from his parents' country. Jordan calls them Native Americans, but Mrs. Wu says they are the Wampanoag people, which is all very confusing. I am still not sure who we are supposed to be thanking, but whoever it is, I would like to thank them for giving us two days off from school.

I roll out my *janamaz*. Each time I touch my forehead to the mat, I pray that the electricity will be on in Karachi when we call Baba.

When I head downstairs, rich, earthy smells greet me from the kitchen. They are not Pakistani smells, but my mouth waters all the same. Hira has settled on the couch in her fuzzy bathrobe and rabbit slippers and is watching something on TV with a loud band playing.

"Look!" Hira calls to me in English. "It's the Macy's parade." She points to the TV.

"Macy's?" I plop into the chair across from her. Giant, colorful balloons shaped like animals and people and characters from movies hover above a street parade, dipping and bobbing in the wind.

"Macy's is a big store." Hira points to the television. "The parade is in New York City."

This is another fact my little sister knows that I don't. And she says it in English. I remember the saying Jalaal told me about: "as American as mom, baseball, and apple pie." Maybe it should be "as American as Hira, baseball, and apple pie."

The announcers on TV seem very happy about this parade. I can't always follow what they say because they talk so fast, but I am fascinated by the big, flat, decorated trucks. Uncle says that the flat trucks that don't float are called floats, which doesn't make sense. I wonder what it would be like to ride on one of the balloons—up, up over the ocean, then across the land to Baba.

When the phone finally rings, Hira grabs it first. Listening to her talk with Baba, I realize she uses as many English words with him as she does Urdu. Baba speaks English sometimes at work, but I think his English must have the same holes mine does. Words like *Macy's* and *floats* and even *Thanksgiving* might be new for him.

I try to wait patiently for my turn, but it's hard. Just when I think Hira is finally going to hand me the phone, she says, "Daddo!" Now she's talking to my grandmother? Hira shouts to us, "I'm on speakerphone," like that makes her someone important.

But as she talks, her smile fades to a frown as she struggles with Urdu words. I have never heard Daddo use English; I don't think she knows how.

Hira starts a sentence in Urdu, covers the mouthpiece, and whispers, "How do you say *turkey*?" After a few more sentences, she asks, "What's the word for *report card*?"

She looks at me in frustration. Finally she hands me the phone.

"Hello!"

"Bilal!" A chorus of my relatives' voices comes through the line. "Thanksgiving *Mubarak*!" Baba says, and we both laugh at our own version of *Happy Thanksgiving*.

140

Since I am on speakerphone, their questions tumble out all at once, and I try to keep track so I don't miss any.

"How is school?"

"Is your baseball team winning?"

"Are you getting enough to eat?"

That last question comes from Daddo.

I tell them school is fine. I don't tell them it's still hard for me to keep up in English, or that I am behind in reading. Or that when I start to write something on a blank page, sometimes I still put my pencil on the right-hand side of the paper before remembering I must start on the left.

I decide to stick with baseball. "The season is over now—it's getting too cold to play outside. We start again in the spring."

Baba tells everyone that I play on a team called the Cardinals and I am a great pitcher and a medal winner for most improved. Then he tells them what a pitcher is, because it's a little different from the bowler in cricket.

Daddo interrupts him; she is the only one who ever does that. "Bilal? Are you there?"

"Yes, Daddo, I am here."

"Do you like this baseball? Is it fun?"

I pause. Sometimes it is fun, but only when I'm pitching. Mostly it's frustrating.

"Yes, Daddo. It's a lot of fun. Baba says when he gets to America, he's coming to all my games."

Lots of murmuring comes over the line, and I can imagine everyone nodding and smiling. I only want to hear Baba say, "Yes! I will be there soon, Bilal, and I will come to every baseball game, like I promised."

He doesn't say this, though, so I ask a different question: "Baba, when can I call Mudassar?"

The relatives' voices stop and then I hear shuffling, followed by Baba's voice, closer now. I can tell I am no longer on speaker.

"Bilal, I know you are missing your friend."

My relatives' murmurs start up again but then fade. I think Baba is moving into another room to talk to me.

"I haven't talked with Mudassar since we left—almost five months!"

"I know, Bilal *jaan*."

"But *I* don't know. I still don't know why because you won't tell me."

Baba sighs and is probably nodding and running a hand through his hair. "I will do my best to explain."

I grip the phone.

"I am sad to say that Mudassar's father did something wrong, Bilal. He took money from some of our clients at work."

Now I move into the darkened front room, away from the others so I can hear Baba better.

"Is he—is he in jail?"

"No, Bilal. It is my word against his, which makes it complicated. He is saying that I am the one who took the money."

"But you would never do that!"

"Of course I wouldn't. But I have to prove that he is the guilty one, not I."

I nod even though Baba can't see me. "Is that why you can't come here?"

"That is why I cannot come there yet. But I will come, Bilal, I promise."

My mother rests her hand on my shoulder, and I know it's

her turn to talk. She steers me back to the family room and nudges me toward my sister, who looks miserable, slumped on the couch. I sit next to her.

Hira is too little to understand the real reason Baba can't come to America yet. I still can't believe Mudassar's father would do that to Baba. They were best friends, like Mudassar and me. Is Mudassar still my best friend? What is his father saying about my family? Maybe we're not friends anymore.

Hira leans her head on my shoulder and sniffles. "Bilal?" Her voice is quiet. When she looks up, her eyes brim with tears. "I don't know all the words anymore."

"That's okay—you'll remember when Baba gets here."

Her bottom lip quivers.

"Besides, Hira, you can teach him all of your English words."

Her face brightens. "I could do that, couldn't I?"

I nod as Humza toddles by, grabbing for the phone Ammi holds out to him. "Say hello to Baba!"

Humza puts his ear to the phone, and I can hear Baba's jolly voice coming through the line, but after a few seconds, Humza loses interest. He drops the phone on the carpet and wanders toward Hira and me.

"Lal!" Humza shouts. He climbs into my lap, reaches for Hira's braid, and stuffs the end of it into his mouth. Hira gently pulls it back and tickles his cheek with the tips of her hair, and he laughs. Ammi comes and puts the phone back up to Humza's ear. He pushes it away and grabs Hira's braid again.

Ammi walks away, still talking with Baba. "He's playing with Hira. I'll put him on next time so he can hear your voice."

I realize a truth about my siblings. Not only is Hira forgetting Urdu, but Humza is forgetting Baba.

When the table is set and the food is ready, Auntie calls us into the dining room. Candles flicker, the light bouncing off plates heaped with food, most of which I don't recognize. Auntie names them for us: *mashed potatoes, stuffing, cranberry sauce, green-bean casserole, candied yams, crescent rolls, gravy,* and *turkey.*

The turkey looks like ones I've seen on TV, except this one is *halal*; Ammi and Auntie bought it at an Afghan butcher shop.

Uncle lifts his hands as if he is holding an open Koran, and we do the same. He says, *"Bismillah hir-Rahman nir-Raheem,"* reminding us of Allah's grace and mercy. Looking at the strange food on the table, I am hoping Allah will have mercy on my taste buds. We each say our own silent prayer. Mine, as always, is for Baba. This time, I also say a prayer for Mudassar.

Auntie beams as she looks at the table. "We eat Pakistani dishes for many meals, but this is one time of year when we eat a traditional American meal." She holds up a crescent roll. "This shape reminds me of the crescent moon on the Pakistani flag, the symbol of progress." Auntie smiles. "So we do have a little bit of Pakistan on our American table."

I'm not sure where to begin. I decide it's safest to start with the bread. I take a roll and spread some of the dark sauce called *cranberry* on top, then take a bite. I expect it to be sweet, but it's tart instead.

Auntie laughs. "Bilal, the cranberry sauce is for the turkey. But I think it's a good idea on bread, too."

The meat? Why would anyone put fruit sauce on meat? I decide it's fine on bread and finish my roll.

My favorite is definitely the mashed potatoes with gravy, and in second place is the turkey. I'm a little nervous to try the stuffing, because who knows what's in it? It is a mishmash of colors, like the fall leaves that have already blown away. When I taste this stuffing, I decide it's okay. But I don't ask for seconds.

Auntie brings out something called *pumpkin pie* for dessert. She lets us spoon as much whipped cream as we like on top of our slices, and I can't wait to try it. But when I take a bite, I have to work hard to fake a smile and say, "Mmm!" as I chew and force myself to swallow.

I must not be a very good actor, because Auntie says, "There may be a bit of *jalebi* if anyone is interested." She stands and winks at me before heading into the kitchen.

When she comes back, I dig into the crispy sweetness of the curly noodles.

Jalaal takes a piece and says, "I thought this was going to be an all-American meal." He grins at his mother, and her eyes twinkle.

"If you'd rather not eat the *jalebi*, I'm sure I can find someone who will want seconds."

I raise my hand hopefully, and everyone laughs.

When our stomachs are full and our plates empty, Uncle says, "*Alhamdulillah*," to praise Allah for the food. He also thanks Auntie, who thanks Ammi for making the *jalebi*, who thanks Hira for fluffing the mashed potatoes with a fork, and somehow Jalaal and I get thanked for what we'll be doing later, which is taking out the trash.

Auntie smiles and turns to Jalaal. "Bring the markers, will you?"

Jalaal disappears into the kitchen and returns with a plastic cup filled with markers of different colors.

"Thank you, Jalaal. Why don't you clear the plates while I explain this part?"

As the plates and platters are taken away and Uncle turns up the lights, I see that the tablecloth designs are not designs, they're words—some in English and others in Urdu.

Auntie explains. "I got this idea from a neighbor when we first moved to America. Here—take one." She passes around the cup of markers. I choose a blue marker, the color of a Karachi sky in November.

"Every year, we each write something for which we are thankful. We try to write something different each year."

Ammi smiles. "What a lovely idea. It will be difficult to choose only one thing."

If I had had to do this last year, there are a million things I could have written: cricket, Mudassar, my family being together. But last year, I would not have thought about being thankful for having my family together, because we had always been together. It's not one of those things you think about— it just is. Until it's not, and then all of a sudden you wish you had been more thankful.

Hira poises a fuchsia marker in midair. "So it doesn't *have* to be in Urdu?"

"That's right," Uncle says. "It could even be a drawing, if you'd like."

Hira grins and gets to work.

Humza gets a different kind of marker and a regular piece of paper on his high-chair tray.

I uncap my marker and try to look at what others are writing, but I can't tell. I look at what they've written in the past, and I notice there are a lot of baseball things written by the same hand over the last few years. I wonder if Jalaal will come up with something that's not about baseball.

I could write *baseball*, but there are only some parts of baseball I'm thankful for. Actually, just one part—pitching.

Everyone is putting the caps back on their pens, so I quickly write something down:

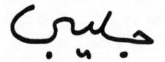

Auntie looks around with a satisfied smile. "Who wants to go first?"

First? We have to say what we wrote?

"I'll go," Hira says. "I wrote *peanut-butter sandwiches.*"

Something American written in English, of course.

"A steady job," says Uncle.

"Family," says Ammi.

"Neighbors," Jalaal says, and I know what he really means is *neighbor*, a red-haired one in particular.

"Allah," says Auntie. She looks at Jalaal as she says this, so she must know which neighbor, too. I bet she's praying about it to Allah right now.

It's my turn, and now I feel silly saying my answer. Everyone said something serious except for Hira. And Humza, who has more marks on his hands than on his paper.

"Bilal?" my mother asks. "What are you thankful for?"

I run my fingers over the word and take a breath. "I wrote *jalebi.*"

Ammi smiles. "I'm glad you liked my dessert."

I grin back. "I liked everything else, too," I say, hoping Allah will forgive me for not telling the truth about the stuffing and pumpkin pie.

The adults seem satisfied with my answer. What I don't say is that *jalebi* tastes more special here somehow. I used to eat it all the time back in Karachi, but I never thought twice about being thankful for it—it was always there. But here in America, *jalebi* tastes like more than sugary syrup and fried batter. It tastes like good memories with friends. It tastes like happiness and holidays. It tastes like home.

# Eighteen

Miss Salinas, our music teacher, is very excited about something she calls the Holiday Sing-Along. Right before winter break, every grade will perform holiday songs from different parts of the world for the parents. I wonder which song we will sing from Pakistan.

She asks how many of us will be celebrating Christmas next month, and almost everyone raises a hand. Jordan doesn't raise hers.

"Okay!" Miss Salinas says. "How many of you will celebrate Hanukkah?"

Five kids raise their hands. Josh calls out, "We celebrate both."

"Right!" Miss Salinas smiles like she's grateful he brought that up. "How many of you celebrate both Christmas and Hanukkah?" Only two kids' hands go up, including Josh's.

"You two are in luck, because this year Hanukkah begins on Christmas Day!" She seems very excited about this fact. "Hanukkah will run from December 25 to January 1."

Now I understand—we'll be singing songs about December holidays. I raise my hand. "In Pakistan, our 25 December holiday is Quaid-e-Azam Day."

Miss Salinas looks surprised. I think she is impressed because I guessed the holiday we will sing about.

"What holiday is that?" Miss Salinas looks interested, but maybe this is not one of the December holidays on her list.

"It is the birthday of Quaid-e-Azam Mohammad Ali Jinnah," I remind her.

Miss Salinas's eyebrows come together, and now I know for sure she does not know about Quaid-e-Azam Mohammad Ali Jinnah. How do I explain?

I remember Jalaal pointing to the old men on American dollar bills. One of them is the father of America, but I cannot remember which one.

Now everyone is looking at me, so I have to say something. "He helped make Pakistan when Pakistan left India."

"Oh!" Miss Salinas tilts her head. "He sounds like a very important person. And Pakistan used to be part of India? How interesting!"

I stare at Miss Salinas, then glance around. None of my classmates have any idea what I am talking about. I guess since I don't know who is the father of America, then maybe it's fair that Americans don't know the father of Pakistan, or that Pakistan and India used to be one British colony. But still.

Miss Salinas breaks the silence. "That leads right into our next holiday. Who celebrates Diwali, the festival of lights?"

That holiday isn't in December; Akash and his family celebrated it about a month ago, near Halloween time.

Miss Salinas holds up her finger like she's ready to count all the kids who celebrate Diwali.

No one raises a hand.

"Okay." Miss Salinas looks around. "How about Ramadan, then?"

I raise my hand; I am the only one.

"Wonderful, Bilal! We'll be singing a Ramadan song, too."

A Ramadan song? In December? This year Ramadan was during the summer. It moves back about eleven days every year, but I'll be old before Ramadan ever falls in December.

"Okay, then!" Miss Salinas's eyes rest on Jordan. "Does anyone celebrate a holiday not on our list?"

Jordan folds her arms and looks at her shoes.

"No? Okay, then, our program is set. Let's begin, shall we?"

Miss Salinas plays recordings of all four songs. Most of the kids sing along to the Christmas and Hanukkah songs—one about a little town somewhere and the other about a clay thing called a *dreidel*. No one sings along with the Diwali song. And the Ramadan song? I've never even heard of it. It's in Arabic, so I don't understand most of it.

Later, when I get off the school bus, I have to jog to catch up with Jordan.

"Wait!"

She looks over her shoulder and slows. "Hey, Bilal."

I fall into step beside her. "You did not raise your hand in music class."

She picks up her pace, and I have to take long strides to keep up.

151

"We celebrate Christmas."

I nod, but I do not understand. Why didn't she raise her hand, then?

"It's just . . . my mom and I celebrate it when my dad comes home."

"Oh." I wish I could say more. Although I don't have all the English words I need, I try anyway. "We left my father one day before *Eid ul-Fitr*—the last day of Ramadan."

Jordan looks confused.

"Ramadan lasts one month, and when it ends, Eid begins. Eid is a big party with your family, your friends. But this year we left Pakistan before we could celebrate Eid, and my father stayed behind."

"That stinks."

"Yes, so much."

"But you got to spend the Ramadan month with your dad, right?"

I think of the three days he was missing, but decide not to tell that part to Jordan.

"Most of the month, yes."

"So that's good—at least you were with him for a whole holiday month."

I shrug. "That was not the most fun part. You are supposed to fast—only eat and drink when the sun is down."

Jordan's eyes open wide. "Wow—you must get hungry."

"That is the point. To understand how people feel who do not have enough to eat."

She nods, and I think she is impressed. "I don't know if I could do that," she says.

"Neither do I, actually."

Jordan looks surprised.

"I have never done the fast before—I have always been too young. This year I wanted to, but Ammi—my mother—said I should wait until next year."

"You lucked out."

I shrug. It's hard to explain that fasting is not a burden; it is something grown-ups do, something I want to do.

Jordan kicks a pinecone, sending it flying into the street. "My mom and I open presents from my relatives—Uncle Matt and Aunt Carol, and my little cousins. My grandparents send gifts, too. But I save one present for my mom and she saves one for me, and we have one present for my dad. When he gets home, we put up a fake tree and open our presents."

Jordan's faraway smile makes it seem like she's watching a movie of her family's Christmas in whatever month they celebrate.

We walk in silence all the way to her house.

Stopping at her front yard, Jordan asks, "Any news about when your dad is coming?"

I wish I knew. "Not yet."

Jordan nods and shifts her backpack from one shoulder to the other. "I bet you'll hear something soon."

As she walks to her door, I think about the idea of having Eid when my father comes back. We could have the same foods. My mother, Auntie, and Hira could get henna designs on their hands. We could go to the mosque and thank Allah for bringing my father back. I wouldn't even care if there were any gifts. Having Baba back would be enough.

✦　✦　✦

The day of the Holiday Sing-Along has arrived, and you'd think Miss Salinas is prepping us for a Bollywood production. She flutters around at our rehearsal, making sure we're all in our places up on the gym stage. The six classes of fifth graders stand on four tiered rows of risers, with the front row on the wooden stage floor.

The gym has been transformed into a "winter wonderland," as Miss Salinas calls it. Strings of tiny white lights drape from the center of the ceiling to the basketball hoops on the four sides of the gym. One entire wall is covered with the snowflakes we made. The silver glitter glued to the snowflakes makes them look like they're sparkling in the sun. From here, you'd never know my ugly snowflake is up there with all of the beautiful ones.

My classmates started making them yesterday while I was in ESL class. I was late getting back to Mrs. Wu's room because Mr. Jacobs had asked me to do a reading test. He thinks I'm doing such a great job in English that maybe I won't even need ESL classes much longer. I couldn't wait to tell Mrs. Wu.

But by the time I got back to class, bits of cut paper were everywhere as kids scurried around the room cleaning up. Jordan showed me how to make a hurried paper snowflake, which reminded me of one of Daddo's lace scarves. But my attempt at paper snow didn't look at all like lace; it looked more like a tattered tissue you'd find on the floor at the end of the school day.

Looking now at the snowflakes up on the gym wall, I can only hope mine is way at the top where no one can read my name. Maybe I should have written it in Urdu letters.

"Bilal?"

I blink. Miss Salinas is looking at me.

154

"I said, let's run through the Ramadan song first." She jabs her thumb over her shoulder at the instruments set up along the front of the stage. The kids standing in the rows below me move aside so I can step down and join the other instrument players. I find the xylophone I'm supposed to play, and sit next to a kid with a silver triangle.

We rehearse the song, and I am glad to say I remember almost all the notes on the xylophone. I just wish we weren't right up front.

When rehearsal is over, Miss Salinas claps her hands. "Bilal," she says to me, "you will be a smashing success!" Then in a louder voice: "I'll see you all back here at one forty-five. Remember, your parents will be attending, so best behavior at all times. Perform like professionals!"

As we walk back to the classroom, I'm surprised to see Jordan at the head of the line. She wasn't on the bus this morning, and I didn't see her come in late; maybe she arrived during my xylophone playing.

When we get back to class, Mrs. Wu has a magnet activity set up for us where we have to build a circuit—she calls it *electromagnetic*. After she gives the directions, our group divides up the tasks. I'm unrolling my copper wire when Jordan leans over her desk, a wide grin stretched across her face.

"Bilal! Guess what?"

Before she can say any more, Mrs. Wu kneels next to Jordan's desk. "I'm so pleased your father is back for a visit!"

"Thank you, Mrs. Wu!" Jordan gushes. Mrs. Wu pats her shoulder and moves to the next group.

I stop, my copper wire half-unrolled, and stare at Jordan. "Your father—he is back?"

She nods so fast her freckles blur. "For five days. He surprised us this morning. He won't be here on Christmas Day, but it's better than nothing."

"This is great," I say, and it is. But it makes me miss Baba even more. Until this moment, I didn't realize that Jordan missing her father somehow helped me—it made me feel like I'm not the only one. But now Jordan's father is here. And Baba is not.

Later, when we file into the gym for the sing-along, I look around for my mother. I think I'll never spot her in this crowd, but then Uncle stands and waves both hands over his head. I smile and send a wave back.

Almost everyone is here—Auntie and Uncle, my mother, and Humza. Jalaal is supposed to come straight here after the high school dismissal bell, but I don't know if he'll make it in time. I try to picture Baba standing there alongside Ammi, but I just can't. I know he is taller than Ammi, but how much taller? How does he stand? How does he walk?

We fifth graders sit and watch all the other grades perform first. When the first graders take the stage, Hira looks like she's right where she was born to be. She curtsies to me, and I smile back. Hira ends up having a small solo part, her high, clear voice floating through the gym. I look back at my mother, expecting to see her wiping away a tear, but instead she's holding up the iPad, filming the concert.

Then it's our turn to sing, and we take our places on the risers. Jordan stands two rows below me, and while I can't tell exactly where she's looking, it's somewhere off to the right. Whichever one her dad is, I wonder if he'd rather be watching Jordan play baseball instead of listening to all of us sing.

We sing our four songs, and I only make a few mistakes on the xylophone during the Ramadan song. With all the voices singing behind me, I hope no one noticed.

After the performance we return to our classrooms, where our families will meet us for dismissal. I'm packing my backpack when my family comes into my classroom, including Jalaal—he made it after all. Hira is already with them, her coat on and her backpack slung over her shoulder.

"Bilal!" Hira lets go of Auntie's hand and rushes over to me as I pull my coat from my cubby. "Did you see me? Did you hear my solo?"

I smile. "You sounded great, Hira."

She beams. "So did you, Bilal. Will you teach me to play that . . . what's that instrument called?"

"A xylophone." I have to admit it's nice to know a word in English that Hira hasn't learned yet.

My mother is near the door, signing me out, and I head over to say good-bye to Mrs. Wu.

"Happy holidays, Bilal!"

"Thank you, Mrs. Wu. Happy holidays to you, too."

Jordan calls Mrs. Wu's name, and I turn.

Even if he weren't standing in between Jordan and her mom, I'd know he's her father. He's got the same freckles and dark hair, although it's so short I can't tell if it's curly or not. I have seen Jordan smile before, but never this big. Her smile matches her dad's.

People say I look like Baba, but I could never really see it. If he were here in my classroom, I wonder if people would say things like "Bilal, this must be your father!" or "Wow—you two look so much alike!"

Jordan introduces her dad to Mrs. Wu, and I turn away. I join my family outside in the hallway, and we head for the car.

One day Baba will come to my American school, and I will introduce him to Mrs. Wu and to Jordan and to Mr. Jacobs, too.

One day.

# Nineteen

If it were anyone but Hira screaming, I would think some-thing was wrong. So when my little sister's shouts carry all the way up the stairs this morning, I just roll over and close my eyes. Until the door bursts open and ricochets off the doorstop.

"Bilal! Jalaal!"

Hira has arrived.

From the muffled grunt underneath Jalaal's covers, I can tell he's now used to Hira's enthusiasm over every little tiny thing.

Before I can ask what she's doing here, my sister scrambles onto Jalaal's bed and yanks the cord to the window blinds. They zip to the top as a Jalaal-sounding "Oof!" and "Ow!" come from under his covers.

Hira stands on Jalaal's bed in front of the window in her Hello Kitty nightgown, triumphant.

I sit up, blinded for a moment by the brightness streaming in through the window.

"Hira," I say, rubbing my eyes, "what are you doing?"

Cupping her hands around her mouth as if there's a chance we won't hear her, she yells, "Snow!" She claps, then points out the window with both hands.

Snow? Snow!

I'm out of my bed and next to Hira in less than a second, my palms pressed against the cold glass.

Jalaal's arm snakes out from underneath his covers, and he grabs his phone from the bedside table. His head emerges next, hair sticking up in every direction, a crooked grin on his face. "School's canceled, little buddy. You can go back to sleep." With that, he rolls over and burrows back under the blankets.

Sleep? Who can sleep?

I have seen photos of snow from the K2 mountain; our Pakistani giant is the second-highest peak in the world. But I have never seen snow that covers houses and cars and trash cans by the curb, or bushes or trees, or . . . Olivia?

"Hey!" Hira calls down to Olivia, who is dressed in puffy warm clothes and is shoveling snow from her driveway. "Wait for me, Olivia!" she calls over her shoulder as she darts out of the room.

Jalaal throws off his covers and sits up. "Let's go check out the snow."

I'm halfway down the stairs when I realize I skipped my *Fajr* prayer. But Uncle sees me and smiles, waving me downstairs.

"Your first snow, Bilal. Let's get outside!"

As I gulp down my cereal, I send up thanks to Allah for the snow and promise not to miss the midday prayer, the *Dhuhr*.

By this time Jalaal has hauled himself out of bed, and he digs out his old snow pants, gloves, hat, and jacket for me.

We spend part of the morning building a snowman. Even Humza helps, bringing over clumps of snow that I help him pat onto the snowman's base. Hira declares our creation to be a snow fairy before running inside to get a tiara, fairy wings, and glitter. Jalaal pats the snowman, shakes his head, and says, "Sorry about that, man."

I pat the snowman, too, and say, "Yeah, man. Sorry."

Ammi decides Humza has already eaten way too much snow and brings him inside to warm up.

Olivia rubs her mittens together. "Who's up for building a fort?"

We've got the walls as high as my waist when Jordan comes by. She surveys our work and declares, "Nice."

"Thanks." I pat down the top of the wall with my snow-encrusted glove and step back to take in our masterpiece.

"Hey, Jordan," Jalaal says, "want to help us out?"

"Sure." Her freckles stand out even more in the winter.

Hira recruits Jordan to sprinkle glitter on the very top of the snowman. Jalaal, Olivia, and I finish our fort, then help Jordan and Hira build another one.

Jalaal raises a corner of his mouth in a mischievous smile. "You know what time it is, don't you?"

Olivia waggles her eyebrows. "Time for a snowball fight?"

Jordan scoops up some snow. "Bring it."

Hira cheers even though I don't think she knows why.

Jalaal explains the rules: "It's simple. The last one hit with a snowball wins. You can leave your fort to get a closer shot, but if you're pinged with a snowball, you're out."

161

He stands midway between the two forts. "I'll referee."

Hira slips her hand into Olivia's glove. "I'm on her team!"

Jalaal smiles and shakes his head at Hira. "You two?" He jabs his thumb toward Jordan and me. "Against the two best pitchers around?"

Hira looks at Olivia. "Are you good at this?"

Olivia laughs. "I've been in my fair share of snowball fights." She looks at Jordan and me. "But these guys? They're going to be tough competition."

Hira thinks about this for a few seconds, then slips her hand from Olivia's and marches over to me. "Let's go, Bilal. You're on my team."

Olivia laughs. "I'll try not to feel insulted."

Jordan and Olivia duck behind their fort, and Hira and I hunker down behind ours.

"What's our plan?" Hira whispers, gathering snow into a lopsided ball.

"We make snowballs as fast as we can, and I'll throw them."

"*I* want to throw them, too." Hira crosses her arms.

I've seen that look before. "Fine. You can throw, just be careful you don't get hit."

But once snowballs start flying, it's not long before Hira scrambles out from behind our fort, a snowball in each hand.

I peek over the top of the fort in time to see Hira and Olivia pelt each other.

"We're out!" Olivia laughs and puts her arm around Hira. I crouch again behind my fort.

Now it's down to Jordan and me.

I'm careful to shift my position after each throw, ducking

behind the snow wall so Jordan can't track where I am. Snowball after snowball flies over the wall, inches from my hat. No matter how fast I make and throw snowballs, more and more fall around me. But when four snowballs fly over my wall at once, I know something is weird.

I peer over the wall in time to see four arms launching from behind the other fort.

"Hey!" I stand and immediately get hit in the chest with two snowballs, icy snow spraying my face.

Giggles erupt as Hira pops out from behind the other fort. "We got you! Bilal is out!"

Jalaal, Olivia, and Jordan stand, snowballs in hand, grinning.

"Four against one?" I say, tossing my snowball up and catching it. "That sounds fair." I smile, then charge their fort.

Snowballs fly until Jalaal begs for mercy and Auntie opens the door.

"Hot chocolate, anyone?" Her smile wavers a little when she sees Olivia.

"Me!" Hira raises her hand and races toward the door. As Auntie helps Hira take off her wet coat, gloves, and hat, Jalaal turns to Olivia.

"Want to come in?"

Olivia glances at Auntie, who is now unwinding Hira's scarf, then looks at Jalaal. He nods.

"Um, sure. I'd love some hot chocolate. Thanks."

Auntie looks surprised that Olivia said yes, but there's nothing she can say about it now.

We arrange our wet gloves and hats and jackets on the fireplace hearth and head to the kitchen, where mugs of steaming chocolate are waiting.

"Wow—are these marshmallows?" Jordan points to a plate in the middle of the table with white, star-shaped puffs.

I can't answer since I don't know what a marshmallow is, but Jalaal grabs one and plops it into his mug. "My mom made these."

Olivia's eyes grow wide. "You *made* these?" She turns to Auntie. "I've never even heard of homemade marshmallows."

Auntie smiles. "They are fun to make, actually. We can't use the store-bought kind because they contain pork."

Jordan's smile fades. "Pork? In marshmallows?"

Jalaal grins. "They grind up the hooves and other parts of cows and pigs to make the gelatin. You can't taste it—"

Auntie raises an eyebrow, and he adds, "I mean, so I've heard."

Jordan grimaces. "Hooves? Ew."

"We don't eat pork," Auntie explains, "so we buy a special kind of gelatin at the store."

Jordan stirs in a marshmallow and takes a sip. "These kind are way better."

"Mmm," Olivia agrees. "I've never tasted marshmallows this good before."

"Thank you." Auntie smiles and places another marshmallow beside Jordan's mug and another near Olivia's.

"Who's up for sledding?" Jalaal asks.

"Sledding?" I ask.

Jordan stares at me, then nods. "Right—this is your first snow, isn't it?"

"Mine, too!" Hira adds.

"You'll love it." Olivia takes her last sip of cocoa.

"How many sleds do we have in the garage?" Auntie asks.

Jalaal stands, spooning out the last of his hot chocolate from the bottom of his mug. "I'll check."

"We've got some, too," Jordan says.

Olivia gathers the mugs and rinses them in the sink. She reaches for the other mugs to rinse them, too, but Auntie turns off the water. "I'll finish up here."

Olivia looks unsure, but Auntie smiles. "Bilal and Hira need some expert sledding instructors. Go on and have fun."

"Thank you." Olivia dries her hands. "The hot chocolate was delicious."

Hira tugs on Olivia's sleeve. "Let's go!"

Ten minutes later we're trudging down the street toward the park. Jalaal and Olivia take turns pulling Hira on one sled, and Jordan and I tote her two sleds behind us.

Jalaal nods at Jordan. "Judging by that snowball fight, it looks like you're keeping up that pitching arm."

Jordan shrugs. "My uncle practices with me sometimes. He's pretty busy with work, though."

"Hey." Jalaal glances at me like I've given him an idea. "Jordan, you should come to the indoor batting cages with us sometime," he says. "I've been meaning to take Bilal."

Jordan grins. "That would be great!"

It would be great; I could learn a lot from her. But why did Jalaal have to suggest a place so public? What if other guys from our team come by?

"Bilal?" Jalaal is obviously waiting for me to speak.

"What? Batting cages? Oh—I mean, great. Or we could maybe practice in our backyard, or yours."

Where no one can see me practicing with a girl—the girl who also happens to be the MVP of a team that doesn't like her.

165

Jordan's smile dims a shade.

"Look!" Hira points toward the park and the hill dotted with kids in colorful winter jackets. When we get to the top, we peer down the steep side, where all the big kids are. There must be fifty people here—sledding down the center of the hill, picking themselves up at the bottom, or pulling their sleds back up for another run.

Jalaal tells Hira she'll have to stick with the gentler hill on the other side, and I expect her to protest. But judging by her wide eyes and clenched jaw as she grips the saucer sled, I think the smaller hill is perfect for her.

Jalaal and Olivia offer to stay with Hira so Jordan and I can tackle the big slope.

Jordan stuffs the tops of her gloves into the cuffs of her sleeves and pulls her hat down over her ears. "Wanna race?"

Of course I do.

We each settle into a sled, bits of snow falling from our boots onto the slick orange plastic. I brace my feet against the curved lip of the sled and grab the yellow rope, wrapping it once around my gloves.

"On your mark." Jordan's eyes narrow. "Get set." She looks down the hill. If these sleds had engines, they'd be revving up loud and long.

"Go!" I say, laughing at her surprise as I steal a head start. After all, this is my first time ever on a sled.

She passes me one second later. Her gloved hands paw the snowy ground faster and faster. I do the same, but as I catch up to her, she reaches for the edge of my sled. I yank on my rope to steer the sled from her path, but I lean too far. My sled tips over, spraying snow down the hill and into my face. Jordan's sled speeds ahead, but when she raises her arms in victory, she loses her balance and tumbles into the snow.

"Ha!" I say, throwing a snowball that splats against her knee. She returns a snowball of her own, and soon we're laughing and dodging and it almost feels like the fun I used to have with Mudassar. Only with snow.

My arm is pulled back, ready to let another snowball fly, when I hear my name.

It's Henry and Akash.

"Hey, Bilal," Akash says. He gives Jordan a nod, and her smile disappears.

"Hi, guys," I say, catching my breath.

"So," Henry says. "You want to sled with us?" He folds his arms across his chest.

He doesn't look at Jordan.

"Sure," I say, meaning we can all sled together.

Jordan picks up her sled. "I got to go." She brushes the snow off her jacket.

I want to tell her to stay, but I can see the guys don't want her to. They don't say it, but Jordan must know, too.

She turns to leave.

"Wait!" I hold out her sled.

She shakes her head. "Just drop it off at my house when you're done."

"Thank you," I call after her, hoping she'll change her mind and stay.

She doesn't.

"Come on, man," Henry says. "You'll have way more fun with us."

We sled for another hour, and the funny thing is I don't

have more fun with them; in fact, I don't have much fun at all. As they slide down the hill, they shout things I don't know: words like "*Banzai!*" and phrases that don't make sense, like, "You're going down, sucker!"

Aren't we all going down the hill?

Although I would never admit this to anyone, I wish the guys had never showed up. Sledding was a lot more fun with Jordan.

 # Twenty

It's official: I don't need ESL class anymore. When I left Mr. Jacobs's room yesterday for the last time, he high-fived me on my way out the door. "Bilal! This is it, my man!"

But to tell the truth, I am going to miss ESL. In Mr. Jacobs's class, I felt smart. In Mrs. Wu's class, I still don't understand everything. But Mr. Jacobs says I understand enough. I hope he is right.

Today is a holiday called Valentine's Day, so Mrs. Wu says my first full day in her class won't be a typical one. I was happy to learn we have another holiday, until I found out we don't have a day off from school for this one. Also, it's all about hearts and love, red and pink, and some white paper lace called *doilies*.

In other words, it is a holiday made for Hira.

I had to buy valentines for everyone in my class, sign them, fold them over, and close them up with a sticker. We also had to decorate a box at home to hold the valentines. Mrs. Wu said we could decorate it any way we wanted, so mine is covered with drawings of baseballs and cricket balls.

For my first official language arts lesson, Mrs. Wu brings out a jar of candy hearts. Some kids applaud; others ask if they can eat some. She holds up a hand. "Today we'll be talking about imperative statements."

Impera-what statements? Maybe I left ESL too soon.

"Who wants to choose a heart from the jar?"

Mrs. Wu calls on José. "Choose a heart, but no peeking!"

José dips his hand into the jar and pulls out a pink heart.

"What does it say?" Mrs. Wu leans in closer to inspect the candy in José's palm.

"Be mine." José does not look happy about this message.

"One of the most famous imperative statements ever," Mrs. Wu claims. "Imperative statements are requests or commands." She takes out five plastic containers, one labeled Imperative Statements and the others with blank labels.

She thanks José, then asks for another volunteer. Teah raises her hand.

"Pick a heart," Mrs. Wu says, "any heart."

Teah chooses one that says "Angel." Mrs. Wu holds it up, even though the letters are too small to read. "Imperative statement, or something else?"

I know "Angel" is not a command or request, but I don't know what to call it in English.

"It's a noun," someone calls out.

"Correct, Lucas." Mrs. Wu puts the heart into a different bucket and prints "Nouns" on the label.

Teah sits down, and Mrs. Wu gives each table group a paper cup filled with candy hearts. "You'll be grouping your hearts into parts of speech. Later on, we'll figure out how we'll need to label these other containers."

Our group works together and finds imperative statements like "Hug Me" and "Text Me," but we also find more embarrassing ones, like "Kiss Me." We find nouns with adjectives, like "Sweet Pea" and "Love Bug," and plain adjectives, like "Cute." And then we find some we don't know how to label, including "Hey Babe."

In the end, we each get to keep five hearts to munch on while we do our independent practice: coming up with five imperative statements of our own. Everyone starts on their lists as Jordan leans over and whispers, "We could come up with baseball ones—like 'Play ball!'"

I nod. "Or one I always hear: 'You're out!'"

Jordan laughs, then says, "I think that's declarative, though, not imperative."

Before I can ask her what that means, Mrs. Wu approaches our desks. "Jordan and Bilal, please respect those around you. Group work is over; this is independent work."

My face feels as red as Jordan's looks.

I number my paper from one to five. What can I write for my first answer? While I'm thinking, a candy heart hits Jordan's desk and bounces onto mine. We both look around to see who threw it, but everyone is bent over their papers, scribbling away. Not even Mrs. Wu noticed.

I shrug, and pick up the heart.

It reads "Love Birds."

I don't get it. I think it would go in the adjective/noun bucket, but I don't get the message. Jordan must see my confusion, because she holds out her hand. I give her the candy, she reads it, frowns, then rolls her eyes and shakes her head like it's no big deal.

I somehow come up with five imperative statements, and then it's time for the party. Mrs. Wu sets a cupcake platter, bowls of chips, and bottles of juice on the back table.

"Time to set out your valentine boxes, everyone!" Mrs. Wu even has one of her own, covered in shiny red paper. "Once your box is out on your desk, it's time to distribute your valentines!"

I dig out the valentines from my backpack and start putting them into people's boxes. The store didn't have any valentines about cricket, so I got some baseball ones instead.

Once we finish, we get our food and open our boxes. Mine has a jumble of small white envelopes, some with candy or pencils taped to them. Others are folded over and closed with stickers.

Jordan holds up my card, a picture of a baseball that reads "Have a ball, Valentine!"

"Thanks," she says, grinning.

I dig through the box and find the one from Jordan—a picture of a baseball mitt that reads "You're a catch, Valentine!" I don't really get it, but I smile at the way she signed her name in bubble letters; that must have taken a long time. At the bottom, she's written "Practice today—my house?"

I nod. "I definitely need help with my curveball."

Jordan gives me a thumbs-up.

On the bus ride home, I slide into the seat with Akash, across the aisle from Henry. "So, did you guys get anything good at your party?" Akash asks, pulling a valentine from his bag. "I love these." He rips off the miniature chocolate bar taped to the valentine, tosses the card back into the bag along with the wrapper, and pops the chocolate into his mouth.

Henry takes out his bag, and I open the lid to my box. Akash peers inside, rummages around, and pulls out a lollipop. "These are good," he says through a mouthful of chocolate. "I like the bubble gum in the center."

I'm about to say he can have it when the bus goes over a bump, and some of my valentines spill into the aisle.

Henry reaches down and picks them up.

"Thanks." I hold out my hand for the valentines, but Henry pauses, reading one of the cards—the one from Jordan.

He raises an eyebrow. "You guys practice together?"

I wish he would keep his voice down. I glance back at Jordan who sits two seats behind us, reading a book.

I snatch the valentines from Henry's hand and stuff them back into my box.

Akash leans over to look at Henry. "Who practices together?"

Henry nods in Jordan's direction. "Jordan and Bilal." He looks like I've just punched him.

Akash shakes his head. "You practice with her? Why?"

I should say because she's a good pitcher, and because I have fun with Jordan.

But Akash says, "She took Henry's spot on the team, man."

Jordan looks up from her book. She glares at Henry.

I guess he could say that I took his spot, too. I know how much Henry wants to be a Cardinal, but it's not Jordan's fault that he will still be a Phoenix in the spring. Maybe next fall he will have a better tryout.

"So is it true?" Akash asks. "Do you guys practice together?"

173

I turn toward Akash so Jordan can't see me. In a low voice, I say, "Nah, she just wrote that." I shrug, hoping Henry will believe me.

My lie seems to satisfy Akash.

Akash leans out into the aisle. "Maybe we should all practice, though—the season starts up again next month."

Henry stays silent.

I don't look back at Jordan. When I get off the bus, Akash watches me through the windows. Without waiting for Jordan, I head up the sidewalk. When the bus finally pulls away and I know the guys can't see me anymore, I turn. But Jordan isn't walking behind me. I recognize Coach Matt's pickup truck pulling away from the curb with Jordan in the front seat.

I stop by Jordan's house later. As soon as she answers the door and folds her arms, I know she knows.

I pray to Allah she didn't hear my ugly words on the bus. Maybe she only heard what Henry and Akash said.

I force myself to look at her, even though she might hate me. I can picture her handwriting on the valentine card, and I hope the invitation still stands.

"Um, do you still want to practice?"

Jordan tilts her head. "Nah," she says. "I just wrote that."

And she goes to close the door.

"Wait!" I put out my hand, and she almost closes my fingers in the door.

"Take your hand away."

"Okay, but can you listen first?"

She appears to think about this for a few seconds. "Fine."

I take my hand back, relieved to still have my fingers. "I am sorry for my words on the bus."

She tilts her head and narrows her eyes. "So why'd you say that?"

I take a deep breath, but it doesn't help me think of the right words to say.

When I don't answer, she says, "I'll tell you why." She unfolds her arms and puts one hand back on the doorknob and the other on her hip. "It's because you don't want to be seen with me. Because I'm a girl, and obviously everyone on the team has a problem with that."

I open my mouth, but nothing comes out.

Jordan shakes her head. "I thought you were different. You didn't really fit in, either. I thought we could be friends."

I find my voice. "But we are friends."

She raises an eyebrow. "Yeah, when no one else is around. I don't need friends like that."

I think I see her eyes go shiny, but she looks down before I can tell. Two seconds later she looks back up again, and I think I must have been mistaken.

"I only practiced with you because I could tell you needed it."

Her words sting. I think of the times we laughed with Coach Pablo during the pitching clinics. But now I wonder if she was laughing at me instead of with me.

I slide my hands into my jacket pockets. "Well, you do not have to feel sorry for me anymore."

And with that I turn and walk back down the front walk. When I reach the sidewalk, I stop. Maybe I should try to apologize again. Jordan is right—she doesn't need friends who don't want to be seen with her. But I also don't need friends who feel sorry for me.

I walk all the way home without turning around.

I tell Ammi I have homework to do, and take the laptop up to my room. But what I really need to do is talk to Baba. I double-click the Skype app and go to Baba's icon, which says Offline. I try calling on the regular phone, but the power must be out again in Karachi, because a recorded message says, "The number you have dialed cannot be reached at this time."

I close the laptop, fold my arms on top, and lay my head down. I don't want to reach a number; I want to reach Baba. And not only "at this time," but all the time. Every day.

# Twenty-one

I can tell by the way Coach Matt and Coach Pablo grin at each other that the news is good. I'm seated in the bleachers, waiting to warm up for my very first Cardinals practice, my arms folded against the chill of this gray, March day.

Coach Matt rubs his hands together. "All right, folks, time to listen up!"

We all quiet down.

"We've got some good news—an exciting event coming up for the team."

I wonder if Jordan knows what this news is. Living with Coach Matt, maybe she overheard something. But she's still not talking to me, so it doesn't matter.

"We've got a shot at an exhibition tournament where some bigwigs will be watching us play."

Bigwigs?

"And that exhibition game will be played at . . ."

Coach Matt and Coach Pablo grin at each other before saying together: "Nationals Park in Washington, DC!"

Cheers erupt, and even the coaches can't quiet us down. Nationals Park! Wait until I tell Jalaal!

Coach Pablo waves his arms up and down to get everyone quiet again. "We thought you'd all be excited."

Coach Matt nods. "There's a push to include some new sports in future Olympic Games. At the moment, baseball is not an Olympic sport."

There are choruses of "What?" and "Why not?" and "That's not fair!"

Coach Matt raises a hand. "I know. Hard to believe. Baseball became an official Olympic sport in 1992, but we got kicked out in 2012."

Coach Pablo looks disgusted.

"But we are not going to sit around and feel sorry for ourselves." Coach Matt shakes his head. "There are two groups working together on this—one is trying to get baseball back on the Olympic docket."

Coach Pablo glances at his clipboard. "And the other group is trying to do the same for a sport called cricket."

I freeze. Akash nudges my arm, and I shoot him a grin.

"One problem with baseball and cricket in the Olympics is that the games can take a long time."

"So what?" Jack says. "That just means there's more greatness to watch."

Coach Matt and Jack fist-bump. "Good point, Jack. There's one version of cricket that only lasts about three hours, instead of several days."

Carlos looks at me. "Days?"

I shrug. Why is that so surprising?

I've only seen Nationals Park on television, when Jalaal and I watched the games last fall. It looks huge. What would it be like to play there?

"So how does it work?" Jack asks.

"The Cardinals have been selected as one of ten top teams in the region," Coach Pablo explains. "If—when—we make it to the semifinals, the top two teams will face off at Nationals Park."

"We've got our work cut out for us," Coach Matt adds. "The team from Loudoun has been selected for the tournament, too."

Everyone groans except for me and Jordan.

Coach Pablo holds up a hand. "I know—they beat us last year for the state championship. But I think we've got a good shot at winning this. Whoever clinches that exhibition game travels to Toronto this summer for the final game against the Canadian semi-final winners. All expenses paid."

"There's only one catch." Coach Matt looks serious.

What does he mean? Only one catcher? We always play with one catcher.

Coach Matt scans our faces before he speaks again. "If we win, the trip would be a ton of fun—no doubt about it. But if we win at Nationals Park, the final game will take place in Toronto on July fourth—the same day as the state championships here at home. If we do qualify for the state finals game but go to Toronto instead, then we forfeit the state title."

There is too much to think about. Everyone else must feel the same way, because we have the worst practice we've ever had. Coach Pablo says we need to focus, and we are; just not on what's happening on the field.

When Jalaal picks me up after practice, I fling open the car door and blurt out, "The Cardinals might play at Nationals Park!"

Jalaal's eyes widen. "Your Cardinals?"

"Yes!" I get in and pull the door shut, tossing my bag in the back and high-fiving Jalaal.

I fill Jalaal in on what the coaches said.

"Man, Bilal! You playing at Nats Park."

"Only if we make it through the playoffs. Just the top two teams get to play the exhibition game." I can see Jalaal is happy for me, but I think he must also be a little envious, so I add, "It's only for kids twelve and under. They're trying to get more countries to start up cricket and baseball teams for kids, so people will want to see these sports in the Olympics."

Jalaal nods. "So you have to convince a bunch of government diplomats that baseball is a good thing."

"And we will," I answer.

"Your dad will be so psyched if you get to play, Bilal! If you do, I'll film it for him."

"Thanks, Jalaal."

But we won't need a video if Baba can be there for real.

When we get home, I grab my bag and head inside, an idea forming in my head. If Baba knows I might be playing at Nationals Park, maybe he'll hurry up and try to come sooner. I probably won't get to pitch in a game that important, not unless Jordan is sick. But at least I'll be there in the dugout.

Out back, Ammi and Auntie are sitting on the swing, talking. Auntie's hand pats my mother's arm. I slide open the glass door, and Auntie stops mid-sentence.

I tell them how I might get to play at Nationals Park, but

their reaction is not like Jalaal's. Even though they're both smiling, their eyes look tired.

"Bilal, this is happy news," my mother says, but her voice sounds forced.

I look from one to the other. "Can we call Baba and tell him? I know it's late, but he won't mind."

My aunt's eyes dart to my mother's face for only a second, then she looks down at her hands.

"Not at this hour, Bilal. Daddo needs her sleep."

I sigh, but I know Ammi is right. "Did you talk to Baba this morning?"

My mother stands. "He's doing fine, Bilal. He'll be glad to hear your news."

My aunt rises, too. "We'd better get dinner started."

The door closes, but before they head into the kitchen, my mother turns and looks at me. Her smile is sad, and I wonder what she and Auntie were talking about.

I bring my bag up to my room and find Jalaal at his desk, the computer screen glowing. "Hey, Bilal, take a look at this."

He's got a website up about the exhibition.

"Wow." I lean over to get a better look at the big, gleaming stadium.

Jalaal scrolls down, past words and photos of kids playing baseball and cricket. He stops about halfway down and touches the screen with his finger. "Look at the list of the VIPs."

"VIPs?"

"Very important people."

"Oh." The diplomats. I lean in closer. On the VIP list is a name I've heard since before I ever started playing cricket: Omar Khan.

I stand up. "What? *Omar Khan* is going to be there? But he's not a diplomat."

Jalaal clicks on Omar's name, and a new page opens. "It says although his cricket-playing days are over, now he's a politician. He wants to be prime minister of Pakistan."

I don't really care why he'll be there—he'll be there! At Nationals Park. Baba won't want to miss this game. He has to come now. He has to.

# Twenty-two

The next day at the park when I tell the guys about Omar Khan, Akash is the only one who understands.

"What?" Akash stops the basketball mid-dribble and lets it bounce off his shoe and bump-roll away. That's how surprised he is.

Henry chases down the ball. "Who's Omar . . . whatever-his-name-is?"

"Khan," Akash and I say together.

"He is only the very best cricket player in all of the world," I say.

"I don't know about that," Akash says. "But he was captain of the Pakistani team that beat India way back in the nineties."

"And he did it when he was thirty-nine," I say.

Henry shakes his head. "Man, that's old. He must be pretty good."

"He's good," Akash allows.

183

"He's the best," I say. "But now he's too old to play cricket, so he wants to be prime minister of Pakistan."

Henry takes a shot at the basket and misses. "What's that?"

"It's like the president," Akash says, jogging to retrieve the ball. "Hey!" He waves at a kid, a boy who joined my ESL class right before I left.

The boy waves back and jogs over. "Hello, Akash!"

Akash passes him the basketball. "This is Ravi—he's from India."

"Then you know who Omar Khan is, don't you?" I ask.

Ravi nods like it's common knowledge. I like Ravi already.

I tell Ravi how Omar Khan is coming for the exhibition game, but I can tell he isn't following my English. He nods and smiles, but his eyes look a little panicked. I recognize that look.

I want to stay and explain so that Ravi understands, but I need to go finish my homework. We all leave except for Ravi, who heads up the hill to join a kid with a kite.

As soon as I get home and open the front door, Jalaal's voice trails down the stairs. "It's not fair! You never let me do anything."

"That isn't true." Auntie's voice simmers with anger.

"But she's nice. You'd like her if you'd just give her a chance."

"It's not a matter of liking her. She seems very nice."

"Then why can't—"

"Jalaal, that is enough." Auntie's voice is like steel. "I will not discuss this any further."

Furious footsteps pound down the stairs, and I back out the front door, pretending I'm just now coming in so they won't know I was eavesdropping.

184

Jalaal brushes past me and out of the house without a word, leaving the front door wide open in his wake. Auntie nods once to me as she comes down the stairs, her eyes avoiding mine. She rounds the corner and heads down the hall to the kitchen, her *dupatta* trailing behind her like an angry serpent.

My mother calls my name as she comes around the house from the side yard, clipped daffodils in her hand. I sink onto the porch swing and she joins me.

"Better to give them some privacy," she says.

"Auntie looked really upset. So did Jalaal."

My mother sighs. "This is a difficult age for him."

Next door, Olivia's yellow car pulls into the driveway. The daisy hubcaps slow from a white, spinning blur to petals. She steps out and waves, and my mother and I wave back.

I give the swing a gentle push with my foot. "They were arguing about Olivia, weren't they?"

My mother studies my face like she's trying to figure out if I'm old enough to hear what she has to say.

I decide to show her I am old enough. "Jalaal wants to be Olivia's boyfriend, I think."

Ammi bites her bottom lip, and I think she's trying not to smile.

"You have always been very observant, Bilal."

"I am right?"

My mother pushes our swing with the toe of her tennis shoe against the floor of the wooden porch. "It's really none of our business, Bilal."

"But if it were our business . . ."

Ammi raises an eyebrow.

". . . then why would Auntie be so mad at Jalaal?"

Our swing sways back and forth six times before she answers. "It's complicated, Bilal. Jalaal is—we are—Muslim. Olivia is not."

I frown. "So he has to have a Muslim girlfriend?"

"Auntie prefers that he waits to have any girlfriend until he is older."

I think about the Valentine's Day party when someone threw the "Love Birds" heart at Jordan and me. Yuck. I don't want any girlfriend, Muslim or not.

I decide to change the subject. "When can we call Baba?"

My mother glances at her watch. "I'll try to phone him tomorrow."

When I'm at school, of course. I'm always at school when he calls. And on the weekends, our calls usually don't go through.

My mother seems to guess my thoughts. "At least his letters come fairly regularly."

Baba wrote his first letter to us one day months ago when the power was out and he couldn't connect to the Internet. I told him that I liked holding something that I knew he had touched, so now he sends both old-fashioned letters and emails.

Ammi stands. "Should we see if one arrived today?"

"I'll check." I race to the mailbox, pull back the little door, and slip my hand into the cool metal box. I pull out a stack of envelopes, my heart full of hope as I flip through each one. When I get to the second-to-last envelope, I close my eyes and take a breath. Then I peek. It's not from Baba.

My mother watches me from the swing. When I shake my head, her shoulders droop.

I climb back up the porch steps, and my mother stands. "I think we can go in now. Auntie has had some time to cool down."

In case Auntie needs extra cooling-down time, I head upstairs. It's nice to have the room to myself. When Jalaal comes home, he'll probably need some cooling-down time, too, and I'll have to go somewhere else.

I'm only halfway done with my homework when Jalaal slips into our room, eyes on his phone.

"Hi, Jalaal." I didn't even hear him come home.

I expect to see storm clouds in his eyes, but he's actually wearing a lopsided grin.

"Hey, little buddy."

I put down my pencil. "Is Olivia your girlfriend?"

Jalaal looks up from his phone. He shoots a glance at the door, then strides over and closes it.

"It's complicated." He runs a hand through his hair.

I nod like this is news; I feel guilty for overhearing his argument earlier with Auntie.

Jalaal lowers his voice. "Can you keep a secret?"

"Of course." I inch closer to the edge of my chair.

"I want to ask Olivia to prom."

"What's prom?"

"It's this big, formal high school dance."

That's it? That's the big secret? That doesn't sound so great. But I can tell Jalaal thinks it is.

"Do you think she'll say yes?"

Jalaal shrugs. "I think so. At least, I hope so."

I wonder how he's going to do this if his mother won't let him have a girlfriend. "When are you going to ask her?"

"Prom's still a few months away. I've got time."

I nod, even though I have no idea how much time he needs before he has to ask her.

Jalaal looks lost in thought, but finally he blinks. "I just need time to convince my parents to let me go. Especially my mom."

"You can do it, Jalaal."

There's no way he can do it. Auntie sounded mad.

He stands. "Sometimes, little buddy, you have to take matters into your own hands." He pulls notebooks from his backpack, sits at his desk, and clicks on his reading lamp.

I glance at his phone sitting next to his books. I wish I had my own phone so I could call Baba at school, when he's home and awake.

Jalaal said I have to take matters into my own hands. What I really have to do is take a phone into my own hands, put it in my backpack, and take it to school . . .

. . . to call Baba.

Twenty-three

Convincing my mother to let me take her phone to school has not been easy. But my opportunity comes sooner than I expected. Today I have baseball practice after school, but Jalaal also has a dentist appointment and can't pick me up. Since my mom doesn't have a car here in America, Auntie has to pick me up. She also has a million errands to run. We've been running overtime with the Cardinals getting ready for the exhibition tournament, so I never know what time practice will finish. I told her I could just call her when practice is over, and she called that idea very efficient.

When I get off the bus at school this morning, I am sure my phone is well hidden in my back pocket.

Until Akash says, "You got a phone?"

My hand flies to the phone, and I shove it deeper into my pocket.

189

"It's my mom's." I glance around to make sure no one heard him before remembering that I haven't done anything wrong. Not yet, anyway.

All throughout the class morning meeting, the only thing I can think about is calling Baba. I've heard Jalaal say he can never get any reception at school, which means I'll have to call outside at recess. That'll be nighttime in Karachi, but not so late that my phone call will wake anyone up.

When recess time finally gets here, I'm the first one out the door. I've already picked out a place I can go to talk to Baba where no one will see me—behind Mr. Jacobs's trailer classroom. It's risky, because although I am hidden from the playground, I still have to keep my voice down in case Mr. Jacobs spots me.

I take my time walking there, even though I want to sprint. When I finally slip into the shadow of the building, I let out a breath and pull out my mother's phone. Baba's number isn't in her phone's memory, because we always call with the house phone. But of course I know it by heart; it used to be my phone number. I touch the screen to wake it up, tap in the numbers, and wait. At first I think my call has not gone through. What if the power is out again? But then the familiar ring sounds. It's a Pakistani phone ringing—three quick, gurgling rings—different from an American ringtone.

"Hello?"

"Daddo?"

There is a moment of silence, then my grandmother asks, "Bilal *jaan*? Is that you?"

Her voice sounds happy and suspicious at the same time.

I glance around to make sure I'm alone.

"Yes, Daddo, it's me, Bilal."

Another beat of silence. "What time is it there?"

I sigh. "It's one o'clock, Daddo. How is your health?"

I can't just ask to speak to my father right away, or else she'll think something is wrong.

But my grandmother's curiosity behind my call is so strong that she doesn't even answer my question about her health— no complaints about her knees or a headache or anything like that. I think she knows that until I talk to Baba, she won't find out why I'm calling.

"I'm putting your father on the phone."

"Bilal?" Baba sounds worried. "Aren't you supposed to be at school? Are you sick?"

I peek around the corner. "No, I'm not sick at all. In fact, I have some good news—it's baseball news!"

I hope he doesn't notice I ignored his first question.

Baba lets out a breath that sounds like relief. "What is your news, Bilal?"

A red kickball rolls past and stops at the opening between the trailers. I press myself against the wall as a kid stoops to pick it up. She doesn't even glance my way. Still, I keep my voice low, which is hard when I feel like shouting from the rooftop, as Mr. Jacobs would say.

"My team is playing an exhibition game at Nationals Park, where the Washington Nationals baseball team plays. And guess who's going to be there? Omar Khan! Not playing, though—he'll be watching. And it's in six weeks and you have to come. You can't miss it, Baba!"

Baba laughs, and I can imagine him holding up his hands in surrender. "That is wonderful news, Bilal. I remember Omar as a good man and an excellent cricketer."

191

"So you'll be here by then?"

"Actually, I have some news of my own."

My heart sinks to my knees. More delays. I grip the phone, willing my voice to not sound sad when he says he can't come.

"I'll be there next week, Bilal—in eight days, actually."

I open my mouth, but no words come out.

"Bilal?"

I find my voice. "Baba, you're coming? Here? Next week?"

"Eight more days. On Pakistan Day." He laughs, and my heart soars. I want to laugh and cry at the same time, but I am supposed to be hiding Ammi's phone and the fact that I am calling Pakistan all the way from Virginia.

"I will bring your cricket bat. You must be missing it."

I shake my head. "I don't need it here, Baba. No one plays."

"We will play together when I get there. I promise."

Talking about my cricket bat makes me think of my old team. "What happened to Mudassar's father, Baba?"

Baba takes a breath before he answers. "He is under investigation now."

"Does that mean he's in trouble?"

"Not yet. But my name has been cleared, and I am now free to leave, praise to Allah."

I want to ask Baba if I can finally talk to Mudassar, but I am almost sure the answer is no. I will ask Baba once he is here. I still cannot believe that I will see him. Eight more days!

"Let me speak to your mother, Bilal. You can put me on speakerphone, and we'll tell her together."

Uh-oh.

"Bilal? Are you still there?"

I swallow. "Yes, Baba. I'm still here. But Ammi is . . . not here."

"Well, when she gets home, tell her we'll Skype this weekend. I wanted to tell you all then so I could see your faces. But when I heard your voice, Bilal, I could not keep it a secret."

Another ball rolls by, this time a basketball. Followed by Mr. Jacobs.

"Bilal?" Mr. Jacobs scoops up the ball. "Who are you talking to back here?"

I freeze.

"Bilal?" Baba's voice calls in my other ear. "Are you still there?"

Mr. Jacobs tucks the basketball under one arm and waits. He doesn't look mad, just curious.

"Um, I have to go, Baba. I will tell everyone this is a Skype weekend."

And I have the feeling I will also have to tell Mr. Jacobs what I am doing on my mother's cell phone during recess. Even so, I cannot stop grinning.

"Can you keep our secret, Bilal *jaan*? I want them to be surprised."

I think of what my mother would do if she knew I was calling Baba from school.

"Yes, Baba. I will keep our secret."

✦　✦　✦

Baba calls us on Skype as promised, and his announcement is met with tears of joy, jumping, and hugging. Humza smiles and claps at our happy faces, then goes back to pushing his dump truck and making *vroom* noises. The rest of us all talk over one another—my mother and Auntie praise Allah, Uncle wipes a tear from his eye with his knuckle, and Jalaal fist-bumps with me. Hira even hugs the computer screen. Once everyone quiets down again, Baba wipes his eye and sighs. "Bilal did an excellent job of keeping our secret."

Ammi's eyebrow lifts. "Secret?"

She turns to me. "You knew your father was coming?"

All I can do is force a laugh.

"How did you know?"

I wish I could say Baba wrote it in one of his letters, but I can't say a lie right in front of him.

Baba chuckles. "Bilal surprised me with a phone call the other day."

Everyone swivels around to look at me.

"We talked a few days ago, when he called to tell me about his baseball news."

My mother narrows her eyes. "Which day was that?"

No, no, no.

Baba shrugs. "It was, what, Bilal? Monday? Around ten o'clock in the evening my time."

"Oh, really?" I can see when my mother figures out the math. She doesn't take her eyes off me.

I sigh. When Mr. Jacobs caught me talking on the cell phone at school, he just told me to put it away—I didn't even get in trouble. I know I won't be as lucky with Ammi. She might be mad about the phone call, but it doesn't matter. Nothing matters.

Baba is coming home.

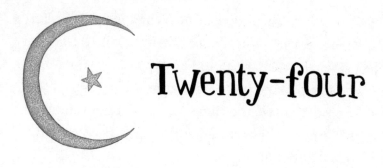

Twenty-four

The house is decorated with Welcome to America signs in Urdu, except for Hira's sign, which reads Welcome Home! in English. Of course.

"Baba knows English already." Hira draws a figure of a smiling girl, arms open wide.

But this isn't really his home. I wonder where we'll live when Baba gets here. Hopefully somewhere close by. Wherever we end up, it will finally feel like home with Baba here.

Baba's plane is supposed to land at 3:40 this afternoon, but we head to the airport extra early in case there's traffic. Auntie and Jalaal stay home because we need to leave room in the van for Baba and his suitcases. Who knows how many he'll have? He promised to bring my cricket bat, and I've already got a place picked out to hang it, right above my desk.

I am surprised by Dulles Airport's towering concrete columns soaring skyward in front of a glass wall, topped with

195

a roof that curves toward the clouds. When we arrived here nearly nine months ago, I never noticed any of these things; I only noticed what wasn't there: Baba.

Uncle finds a parking place right away. I climb out of the van, careful to not crease the signs we made. Hira scrambles out after me, gripping the strings of the brightly colored helium balloons that bob in the breeze.

"How much longer?" Hira asks, skipping ahead.

"Stay beside me, Hira," my mother cautions, pushing Humza in his stroller.

Uncle checks his phone. "He should land in about forty-five minutes."

"But he still has to claim his luggage and go through customs." My mother takes Hira's non-balloon-holding hand. "We'll have to be patient just a little while longer."

I have been patient. For almost nine months. It's a good thing Baba is coming now, because after today I have no patience left. At least not the waiting-for-Baba kind of patience.

We enter through the sliding glass doors, go up the ramp, and pass under a sign that reads International Arrivals.

Scanning the rows of plastic seats, I spot a few empty ones, but I'm too jumpy to sit. Instead I join the crowd at the rope separating us from the passengers emerging through swinging double doors. Other people brought balloons, and some hold flowers, but no one has signs like Hira and I made. I unroll mine to make sure it'll be right side up when Baba sees it.

A crowd streams through the double doors, most speaking a language I don't recognize. I glance back at my mother, who shakes her head and mouths, "Next flight."

It seems like forever has passed when Hira comes up and

leans against me. "Is Baba's plane next?" she asks. I put my arm around her and nod.

"He is going to love your sign." I smile at the crayon-drawn letters.

The double doors pop open, and people in airline uniforms stream out, pulling suitcases on wheels. I recognize the Qatar Airways uniforms from our flight to America last year.

"Hira! He's coming!"

We hold up our signs, careful not to crinkle the paper.

Each time the doors swing open, I stand on my tiptoes to see if it's Baba. I don't know why I do this since we're right up front, but being a few toes taller might make it easier for Baba to spot us as soon as he comes through the doors.

Some people speak Urdu, some Arabic, and some English, but not one of them is Baba. The crowd thins as people wave, hug, and then leave together. Hira's sign is half on the ground, and I remind her to not let it drag on the floor, to be ready for Baba.

The double doors open less and less often, until finally they stay closed altogether.

I turn to where my mother sits with Uncle. He's on the phone, stopping every once in a while to say something to Ammi. Finally he gets up, slides his phone into his jacket pocket, and strides over to the information desk.

My mother looks so alone, even though Humza is with her, asleep in his stroller. Why does Baba have to be the last one off the plane? I want to join her, but when Baba comes through the doors, I want him to see my sign.

"Hira, why don't you go and sit with Ammi? I'll call you over when he comes."

She frowns and hands me her sign. "When you see him, hold up my sign, too, okay? Then I'll come right over and hold it up myself."

I nod and take the sign from her hands, the drawing of the happy girl with her arms open wide smiling up at me. Near the top, where Hira had been gripping the poster, the paper is wrinkled and damp.

I stand with the signs for what seems like another forever, and the doors finally open again. My chest fills with hope, and I lift my sign right along with Hira's. But this time people with different uniforms burst through the doors—a different airline. Not Baba's.

I feel my mother's hand on my shoulder, and I turn.

"When is Baba coming?"

My mother doesn't even try to smile. "He wasn't on the flight for some reason."

Uncle joins us, holding Hira's hand. "Today is Pakistan Day, and you know how traffic is on a holiday. He may have missed his flight. He's probably on the next one." But Uncle doesn't sound hopeful.

There is no way Baba would have missed that flight— Pakistan Day or not. He knew there would be traffic, so he would have left extra early.

Uncle squeezes my mother's hand. "Don't worry, *Baji*. I'm going to take you all home, and then come back and see what I can learn. Perhaps his connecting flight changed and he's coming in on a different airline."

By this time Humza is awake and yells to be let out of his stroller. I give him one of the balloons, and he quiets down again.

I look from my mother to my uncle. "I want to come with you." They shake their heads.

"You have school tomorrow, Bilal." Ammi puts her arm around my shoulders.

Uncle nods. "I may be late. But I will keep everyone posted."

On the way home I hold my rolled-up sign on my lap. Maybe Uncle could bring our signs with him when he returns to the airport. But when I ask him, he says we should hang the signs at home, where my father will see them right when he walks in the door. The balloons dip and rise between Hira and me, like they're trying to cheer us up. It's not working.

My mother or uncle must have already texted Auntie, because when we get home, she greets me with a hug. The house smells like a feast, but the feast will have to wait. I put up our signs with magnets right on the front door, so Baba will see them when he drives up later with Uncle.

But Uncle doesn't come back until way after I'm in bed.

Above me, headlights spread across the ceiling. I throw off the covers and race downstairs. Uncle comes through the door, carrying the signs. He does not bring Baba.

When Uncle sees me, his frown turns to a smile, but his eyes still look worried.

My mother's footsteps pad quickly into the foyer. "Anything?"

Auntie calls from the kitchen: "Hassan?" Then she joins us in the foyer.

Uncle glances at them, then looks at me. "He'll need to rebook his flight, of course."

My mother stares at her brother, like she's trying to read

his mind or send him a message through her thoughts. She nods. "Of course."

Uncle rolls up the signs, hiding Hira's and my pictures and words. He pats my shoulder. "It's late. Time for bed, Bilal."

They start down the hallway toward the kitchen, leaving me at the bottom of the stairs. But I do not move. I do not go upstairs like I am supposed to.

Ammi pauses, turning. "Bilal?"

Uncle and Auntie turn then, too, waiting.

We are always waiting. Waiting for Baba. Waiting for Baba who isn't coming this time.

"It's time for bed, Bilal *jaan*." Ammi's voice sounds tired.

I shake my head and squeeze my eyes shut to keep any tears from leaking out. When I open my eyes, there are our welcome posters tucked under Uncle's arm, which is not where they should be at all. I grab the posters, and Uncle takes a step back in surprise.

Ammi gasps. "Bilal!" but I don't care if I'm in trouble for being disrespectful.

I yank open the front door and find the magnets still clinging to the metal. Tucking my poster under my arm, I unroll Hira's poster, grab some magnets, and slam them onto her drawing. It's not working—the ends are too curled from being rolled up—and the heavy poster board spits the magnets back onto the floor.

My tears are coming even though I don't want them to and now Hira's drawing is a blur of her smiling self with her empty arms open wide and I need more magnets. I pin her poster with one hand and bend to scoop up the fallen magnets, but her poster starts to slip.

Then Uncle's hands are there on the poster, holding it steady. Auntie holds magnets for me to pluck from her hand. Ammi slips my poster from under my arm and rolls it the opposite way so it won't curl. We work in silence until the posters are back in place and my breathing starts to slow back down to normal.

We stand together underneath the porch light, looking at the posters, back where they should be. Waiting for Baba.

Twenty-five

It takes another two days before our call finally gets through to Karachi. Daddo explains that they wouldn't let Baba leave because he didn't have all the right stamps and signatures on his papers. They made him stay at the airport to answer all their questions before they would let him make any phone calls or go back home. Daddo says this is all Mudassar's father's doing. Baba says that Daddo is right.

"He is a powerful man in this city, with many friends who owe him favors." Baba sighs. "But I will find a way."

"Can't we go back home?" I ask.

But Ammi only shakes her head and leaves the room.

I never thought I would be thankful for baseball, but I am. I have no baseball memories with Baba; when I'm out on the field, it is easy to go for an hour or more without thinking of him. I used to try to imagine Baba there in the stands, cheering me on, but lately his face is fading more and more in my mind.

At baseball practice, all anyone can talk about is qualifying for the semi-finals at Nats Park. With each win, the Cardinals get closer to the exhibition game, closer to playing under the big lights, as Coach Matt says.

I don't even care about winning that game anymore. My pitching has gotten better and better, but I'm still nowhere near as good as Jordan. For the big game it will be Jordan out there on the mound, and I'll be sitting in the dugout.

Jack can't stop talking about the game. "My dad works on the Hill, so he's got special tickets for the game, right up front with the VIPs." Jack nods like he's the one who went out and got the special tickets. "It's all about who you know."

I don't know what hill he's talking about until Akash whispers, "Jack's always going on about his dad and Capitol Hill and how important he is in the government, blah, blah, blah." Akash rolls his eyes. "That's how it is with politicians—they're always doing favors for each other, pulling strings."

I still can't think of Omar Khan as a politician. To me, he's still the world's best cricket player. I would give anything to meet him. Maybe I should care if our team wins, because if we do, then we get to shake hands with the VIPs. I'll bring a Sharpie pen and ask Omar Khan to autograph my arm and then never wash it again.

✦ ✦ ✦

The Cardinals make it to the semi-final game, and Coach Pablo says we haven't had a season like this ever. My teammates whoop and clap as we board the bus for Nats Park.

"All right, folks," Coach Matt says after we've taken our

seats. "Let's bring the volume down a notch and focus on the game ahead. Remember, the outcome doesn't matter—as long as you try your best."

Which we all know is a lie. Winning does matter. To the Cardinals, and now to me if it means I'll get to meet Omar Khan. Jordan sits three seats in front of me—alone, of course. I wonder if she's nervous. Probably not.

Our bus drives past the main entrance to the park, where people stream into the gate under a red sign that reads Nationals Park Center Field Gate. Shiny, silver baseballs as big as me line the top of the wall along the street. I see a distorted reflection of our bus in the underside of each giant silver baseball as we move through traffic and turn a corner. This side of the stadium isn't fancy like the front—it looks more like an office building or apartments. We get off the bus and walk through a black gate, the one Akash says the players use. I wonder if this is the gate that Omar Khan will walk through.

I only catch a glimpse of the bright green grass of the field before we turn right through a door leading into the belly of the stadium. Pipes hang far above us, and our cleats echo as we walk past the guest team's locker room. Then we take a left and head up a ramp and out into the sun and the noise of the crowd.

The biggest TV screen I have ever seen rises above the far end of the field. The grass has a checkerboard pattern running through it, and home plate is surrounded by a perfect circle of white sand with that big, loopy *W* right behind it. The coaches lead us down the steps to our dugout, where we sit on a long, wooden bench. It feels kind of like being in a fort, hidden halfway underground with the crowd behind us and the field in front, right at eye level.

The Loudoun team emerges from the other dugout and starts warming up, so Coach Matt calls the Cardinals out to the field, too. I probably don't even need to warm up, since Jordan will be pitching the whole game anyway.

It only takes me a few seconds before I notice the kid on the Loudoun team—a lefty, throwing the ball back and forth with his teammate. I peer through the green fence between the dugout and the field. Coach Matt said Loudoun didn't have any southpaws. I wonder if Jordan has noticed him yet. When Sebastian didn't end up joining the Cardinals, that left only one lefty—me. And Jordan never has trouble striking me out. But a lefty who can swing? I wonder if she's worried.

As I scan the crowd for my family, the announcer's voice booms over the loudspeaker: "Helloooo, baseball fans!"

The crowd cheers and waves in the direction of a gigantic TV screen, while a camera somewhere sweeps across the crowd. The announcer welcomes the VIPs as the camera zooms in on their faces.

I spot him right away—Omar Khan! I can't believe Baba is missing this. The camera pans some more, and there's Jack's dad. He's talking to some of the VIPs, smiling and shaking hands. Jack must be right: it's all about who you know.

That's when the idea hits me like a baseball out of left field.

Omar Khan. He must know people who can get Baba to America.

But how will I get a chance to talk to him? Guys in suits with dark sunglasses surround the VIP section right behind home plate. Would they let a kid in?

Jack can get me in. His dad is practically sitting right behind Omar Khan.

When we finish warming up I ask if Jack can help me. He shakes his head. "I don't have my phone."

There is a phone in the dugout, an old-fashioned one with no numbers on it, so no way to dial. Jack seems to read my mind. "That's a direct line to the press box." He nods at a row of glass windows high above the VIPs' seats. I have to think of another way. Looking around at the security guards, I realize there is only one way to meet Omar Khan: the Cardinals have to win.

A group of men step out onto the field with microphones. They say something about how baseball should still be in the Olympics, but my brain is thinking too hard to listen. Finally they get out of the way so the game can start. According to Coach Pablo, there will be five innings instead of six, since this is an exhibition game and the VIPs are very busy people.

A group of kids in jeans and matching T-shirts comes out and sings the national anthem. I put my hand over my heart like everyone else, which reminds me of Baba's and my secret sign to each other—two pats over the heart.

Once the announcer yells, "Pllllllllaaaay ball!" everyone stands and shouts and stomps their feet. Our team bats first, and Carlos gets to second base on his first hit. When Akash gets a single, though, Carlos is out at third. It goes on like this —one hit, one out, back and forth, with no one crossing home plate. Three outs and now Loudoun is up at bat.

Loudoun cannot win this game. It has to be us.

Everyone scrambles to take their field positions. I'm left in the dugout with the coaches, who haven't taken their eyes off the field.

Jordan's first pitch is so fast, I don't even think the batter knew she'd sent it until it was in Akash's glove. The Loudoun batter hits a foul ball and then a lucky single. The next batter looks fidgety. He should be.

But when Jordan winds up to pitch, she doesn't throw the ball; instead she drops her arm and leans over, hands on her knees. I hope she doesn't throw up.

But no, she stands and pitches. The batter hits it over second and makes it to third before Nate can send it back infield to Jack on third. Safe.

The next batter strikes out, but the kid after him makes it to second, and the kid from third makes it home. Two runs for Loudoun, zero for the Cardinals.

The next kid up is the lefty I saw earlier. I know Jordan hates this, but she can do it.

Or so I thought.

Home run. Two more runs.

Zero to four.

Coach Pablo chews his gum so fast it looks like his jaw will pop any second.

The next inning isn't much better. I spot another lefty on the Loudoun team—that makes two. We finally score a run, but so does Loudoun.

One to five.

We are going to lose the game, but I can't lose my only chance to meet Omar Khan. Once the game ends and everyone is leaving the stands, I'll run over and try to get past the security guards to the VIP section.

We almost catch up in the next inning, but we're still behind by one run at the top of the fourth.

Four to Five.

And at the bottom of the fourth, we're still behind by one. Something is wrong with Jordan. She's taking longer and longer to throw her pitches, and she's off whenever the lefties are up at bat. She's going to cost the Cardinals the game.

Coach Matt waves me over. I stand by his side, but he turns to Coach Pablo instead. "I think it's time."

It takes Coach Pablo a second to look at me, like it pains him to take his eyes off the field.

Coach Pablo shakes his head. "Jordan's doing fine."

He winces when a Loudoun lefty hits a double.

Coach Pablo looks sideways at me now, his jaw working his piece of gum slower and slower until it stops altogether.

Coach Matt nods. "I say put him on the mound." He pulls his gaze from the field and looks at me, searching my face for a confidence I don't feel.

He meets Jordan as she comes down into the dugout, while I stay on the opposite end. I slump onto the bench, my stomach in my throat.

I thought Jordan would look mad, but she just looks empty. Something is definitely wrong, but I don't have time to figure that out now.

Top of the fifth, and we're up at bat. We're still down by one by the time my turn comes up.

Let's just say my turn at bat is over pretty quickly.

Two more outs, one more run, and now we're tied. No one talks as we head onto the field, but we can't help smiling. If this ends in a tie, they have to go to extra innings; only one team gets to go to Toronto. And only one team gets to meet the VIPs. All I need is a few minutes with Omar Khan— enough time to ask for his help to bring Baba home.

Time for the bottom of the fifth; the last half of the last inning.

I take the mound, willing my breakfast to stay in my stomach. But I forget about my stomach when I spot Omar Khan through the safety net behind home plate. I am close enough to see the white crescent moon and star on his green tie—like the flag of Pakistan. He's on his phone, shaking his head. Frowning, he tucks his phone back into his pocket.

I force my gaze back to the batter. He finishes up his good-luck routine with three taps of the bat on home plate, and he's ready to go. So am I.

I let the ball fly.

It's a hit, but he only gets to first.

Next batter.

Strike one.

Again—strike two. But this time the kid on first races to second, catching our shortstop totally by surprise. Safe! This kid really wants to go to Toronto.

Well, so do the Cardinals. I take in a deep breath.

With my third pitch, the crack of wood on the ball sends the batter sprinting toward first. But it's a foul ball—up and behind home plate, and Akash never lets it hit the ground.

Out!

I look over at Omar Khan to see if he is paying attention. He's back on his phone again, looking more unhappy than before.

And speaking of unhappy, Jordan looks miserable, slumped in the dugout with her arms folded and eyes on the ground.

I take a breath. Focus.

The next batter looks as nervous as I feel, and he's out without ever touching bat to ball.

Now all I need to do is strike out one more batter, and we'll go into extra innings. But the next batter gets a single, and the base stealer is now on third. Next to bat is a lefty.

It's up to me. I shake out my pitching arm, then look up into the stands where Omar Khan is shaking hands with the other VIPs as he makes his way down the row. Maybe he's only stretching his legs. A man wearing sunglasses helps him into his jacket.

Omar Khan is leaving.

My heart drops to my feet. I race back to the dugout where my teammates stand frozen, staring at me like I'm crazy.

"Bilal!" Coach Pablo rips off his cap. "What are you doing?"

"Get back out there!" Coach Matt sounds like he's about to pitch me back to the mound himself.

I don't have time to answer. I pull the Sharpie from my bag, scribble on the ball, and then throw the marker down before racing back out to the field.

The words I wrote on the ball seem to pulse against my palm as I take the mound. I study the lefty as he studies me, a smug grin on his face.

I have to strike this kid out to win. I have to get Omar Khan to stay. The crowd whistles and claps, ready for my pitch.

I watch as Omar Khan shakes the hand of the last VIP in his row before jogging down to the men who talked into the microphone before the game started. Flanked by his bodyguards, he shakes their hands and then lifts his own in a final wave.

I glance at the batter, his elbows high, bat at the ready. The crowd is in a frenzy, stomping and waving, their shouts filling my ears. Omar Khan moves out from behind the safety net to shake one more hand.

It's now or never.

I let the ball fly, and it goes right where I want it to—straight into the stands, toward Omar Khan. I can almost see my Urdu words scrawled on the ball as they spin around and around, the ball spiraling, falling, falling.

One of the bodyguards shouts and points, whipping off his sunglasses. Omar Khan turns as if in slow motion, reaches up, and snatches my ball from the air, his fingers closing around my message.

He waves at me and smiles, then tosses the ball to one of his bodyguards as he turns and walks back underneath the Presidents Club sign and into the building.

The great Omar Khan does not look back, and he never looked at the ball.

I stand there on the mound, shoulders slumped, as the Loudoun team goes crazy.

Who knew that pitching the ball into the stands means the other team gets to advance one base?

Which means Loudoun wins. We lose. And I have lost my chance to get Baba to America.

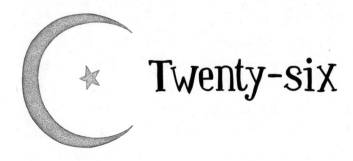

Twenty-six

No one talks to me as we board the bus for home. Everyone talks *about* me, just not *to* me. Except for Jordan, who doesn't talk to anyone. As usual.

Even the coaches avoid me. The only thing Coach Matt said to me when I walked off that field was, "Why, Bilal?" He didn't even look mad, just hurt and confused.

I slide into a seat at the very back of the bus, hoping no one will sit near me. No one does. Akash comes back anyway, and I make room for him even though I don't feel like talking.

But Akash doesn't sit. He stands in the aisle next to my seat. When he speaks, his voice simmers with anger. "That wild pitch? Into the stands? You did that on purpose."

There is nothing I can say to that.

"Traitor." Akash turns and heads to another seat.

The weight of that last word is too heavy. It pushes me

down, and I lie with my back on the seat, looking up at the curved metal ceiling of the bus.

Words like *loser* fly past my ears, but words mean something different to me than they do to my team. *Traitor* is Mudassar's father, who betrayed his very best friend. *Loser* is me, but not in the way my teammates think. I lost more than just a baseball game. I have lost my father.

The bus pulls up to our home field, where our parents wait for us. I stay in my seat until the last player shuffles off the bus.

I look out through the tinted windows as the other families head toward their cars. They're all probably mad at me, too.

When I pass the bus driver, he pats me on the shoulder. "There'll be other games, kid. You guys did your best." He obviously wasn't at the game.

I can see through the windows that the only family left waiting is mine. I spot Hira holding limp pom-poms at her sides. Humza hugs a huge foam hand that reads We're Number One! that's almost as big as he is.

I clunk down the steps. Ammi steps forward, arms open, and hugs me. I close my eyes to keep my tears in, but a few squeeze out anyway. Hira rushes to join the hug, and so does Humza, who has no idea why we're hugging. Auntie wraps her arms around us, followed by Uncle, and even Jalaal joins in the group hug. We are standing this way when the bus pulls away from the curb and rumbles off down the road.

✦ ✦ ✦

I have decided to quit baseball. The Cardinals don't need me; they have Jordan. Jalaal does not take this news well.

"You can't quit!" He throws the baseball extra hard, but I catch it in my glove, no problem.

My only answer is to throw a harder ball back.

Jalaal catches it, no problem. "So you wanted to meet Omar Khan. You got distracted."

I did not tell my family why I threw that crazy ball. I feel stupid for thinking that I could somehow help Baba get here.

"It's not the end of the world." Jalaal sends the ball back, and my glove stops it in midair.

"No, but it's the end of the Toronto trip." I think of how badly everyone wanted to go, including the coaches.

But Jalaal is hearing none of it. "You guys'll be here for the state championship game in July instead. And the Loudoun team won't."

Because they'll be having fun up in Toronto. And even if the Cardinals win the state championship, it won't feel like winning if their biggest competition isn't there.

Jalaal tucks the ball back into my bag. "Just go to today's practice, then see how you feel." He tosses me the bag. "If you still want to quit after today, then quit."

I hate the word quit.

But I'm not going to stay on the team if everyone hates me. I know Jalaal will be disappointed. If Baba were here, he'd be more than disappointed; he'd never let me quit in the middle of a season. He'd say I owe it to the team to play to the end.

"Okay. I'll go to practice. But only for today."

I think I see Jalaal grin as he ducks into the car, but I can't tell for sure. We pull out of the driveway and head down the street. Before we get to the stop sign, Jalaal stops in front of Jordan's house.

214

"What are you doing?"

Jalaal shrugs. "We're giving Jordan a ride. Coach Matt's heading over from work and doesn't have time to swing home and pick her up."

I sigh.

Jalaal nods toward the house. "Go up and knock, will you? We're running kinda late."

I step out of the car and roll my eyes. I should have said I wasn't going to practice at all.

The yellow ribbon on the tree out front is faded and frayed. The pink blossoms fluttering down from the branches only make the ribbon seem more drab.

Before I raise my hand to knock, Jordan yanks the door open. I brace myself for her anger, but she stands there, silent.

So I talk. "I'm sorry about the game."

She doesn't say anything, so I keep talking. "I'm quitting the team."

She shakes her head. "Don't. You're too good to quit."

"But I lost the game."

She folds her arms. "It wasn't my best game, either."

In the hours since my epic error, I had forgotten all about the way Jordan played—almost like she'd been in a daze. "Were you sick?" I ask.

She shakes her head, takes a breath, then stops, like she's trying to decide if she should tell me something.

"It's my dad. He got hurt over there. They don't know how bad yet . . ." Her voice trails off, and she looks at her shoes.

I had been prepared for her to hate me because I lost the game. Now I only wish that were the reason she looks so devastated.

I don't know what to say. She doesn't know Baba can't come to America yet—I never told her because we weren't speaking to each other. My shoulders slump. "I'm sorry—" I begin, but she shakes her head hard enough to set her curls bouncing.

"You don't have to be sorry, because he's going to be fine."

I recognize myself in the set of her jaw. I've become an expert at talking myself into believing Baba will be fine, too. When you are trying to hold yourself together, you don't want to see sympathy on people's faces; you want them to lie and tell you that everything will be okay.

But I'm also sorry about something else.

Jordan grabs her bag and steps out, pulling the door closed behind her. She starts toward the car, but I don't move.

"Wait," I say.

She turns and looks at me.

"I—I'm sorry. About not always being your friend."

She looks at me like she's trying to decide if she believes me or not. Maybe she hates me. Finally she nods. "Thanks, Bilal."

She turns, and I follow her to the car.

We ride to practice in silence. I am lost in a jumble of thoughts—Jordan's father, Baba, me quitting. And not just quitting baseball—quitting hope.

We park just as Akash's van pulls past us. When he gets out, I try to catch his eye, hoping he'll see how sorry I am. But he shakes his head and turns away, heading over to the field where the rest of the team is just hanging out. The coaches stand near the dugout, talking to some men in suits. They're probably all talking about how they hope I don't show up.

When Jordan and I get to the field, everyone's voices fade

to whispers and then to silence. Akash turns his back when he sees me, and Henry never even glances in my direction. Jalaal lingers on the edge of the field, watching like he's waiting to see if I'm okay.

Coach Matt strides over. Instead of telling us to start warming up, he jabs his thumb over his shoulder at the dugout behind him and looks straight at me. "There's someone here to see you."

I turn. My breath catches in my throat.

There, standing in the shadow of the dugout, is Omar Khan.

Twenty-seven

The great Omar Khan strides over, a lopsided grin stretched wide across his face. Two men in suits and sunglasses flank his sides.

He stops in front of me, dust settling on his shiny shoes. I have to lean my head back to look up at him—that's how tall he is. Even though I'm staring right at that famous face, I still can't believe it's him. His face has more lines than I remember, but those eyes are the same ones I have seen in all the television interviews—direct and unwavering, like he can see right through me.

"Bilal?" Omar Khan holds up the ball I threw him yesterday, my Urdu words pinned beneath his thumb. "Is this yours?"

I swallow. "Yes, sir."

Omar Khan speaks to me in Urdu, so none of the other kids understand him—except for Jalaal. The whole team stands silent around us, like if they listen hard enough, they'll understand what's going on.

Omar Khan looks at the ball and reads my message in Urdu: "I need your help." Then he turns the ball so my words stare back at me. "Did you write this?"

"Yes, sir, I did."

Coach Pablo claps once. "Okay, folks, time for practice—let's get moving!"

Coach Matt cuts off the groans of protest. "Hustle, people! Time for warm-ups."

Jordan is the last to leave.

Now it's just me, Jalaal, and Omar Khan. The two guys in suits stand ten feet away.

Omar opens his jacket, resting his hands on his hips. "What kind of help do you need?"

"My father is being kept in Pakistan," I tell him.

Here is the chance I've been waiting for—to meet Omar Khan and tell him all about Baba so he can—what did Jack say?—pull strings to bring him here. Tears of relief spring to my eyes, but no more words come.

Omar Khan seems to understand. He probably gets this reaction a lot.

"Perhaps you would prefer to sit down?" He points to some benches beyond the field.

"Thank you, sir."

Omar Khan motions to the men in suits that they don't need to follow us. They do anyway, but keep their distance. Omar Khan and Jalaal make space for me on the bench between them, and I sit.

Omar Khan's dark eyes focus on mine. "Tell me about your father."

So I do. I tell him everything, from those three days Baba

went missing before my last birthday, to when he was supposed to come on the plane but didn't, and how he can't get to America, all because of Mudassar's father.

When I am finished, Omar Khan is quiet at first. Then he says, "Throwing that ball was a brave thing to do. I suppose your teammates are not very happy with you."

I shake my head. "No, sir, they are not."

He pulls his phone from his suit pocket, and I imagine him making a phone call that will bring Baba here. Instead he looks at something on the screen, then slides the phone back into his pocket.

"May I speak with your family, Bilal?"

I glance at my cousin.

"You can follow us in your car," Jalaal says.

I wish Omar Khan would ask me to ride in his fancy car, but he doesn't.

At home, I hop out of the car just as one of the men in sunglasses goes to open Omar Khan's door. But the greatest cricket player on earth opens his own door. He emerges from the car and adjusts his suit jacket.

Uncle pulls up right behind them, and the men in sunglasses hurry toward his car.

"That's my dad," Jalaal calls to the bodyguards. "I texted him to come home."

Omar Khan holds up a hand, and the men halt their advance on my uncle.

Uncle steps out, his mouth and car door both wide open. Omar Khan follows me over. "Uncle, there is someone I would like you to meet. This is . . ."

"Omar Khan." Uncle whispers the name.

"It is a pleasure to meet you," Omar Khan says, shaking his hand.

Uncle places his hand over his heart, and Omar Khan does the same.

"He's here to help Baba," I tell Uncle, who nods and puts his hand on my shoulder.

"Please," Uncle says, pointing an open hand toward the house. "You are welcome in our home."

We turn to find the rest of my family gathered on the porch. For once in her life, even Hira is silent.

I introduce Omar Khan to Ammi and Auntie. Then I say, all in one breath: "That's why I threw that crazy pitch. I wrote on the ball that I needed Omar Khan's help to get Baba here because Jack says politicians can pull strings, and I think there are lots of strings holding Baba in Pakistan." I take a breath and smile up at Omar Khan. "So he came."

Omar Khan smiles back.

Auntie ushers him in with an offer of tea. I am about to follow when Ammi stops me at the door with a hug. "My smart, resourceful boy." I wish I had told my family about my baseball message to Omar Khan earlier. I thought it hadn't worked. But it has.

I smile. Everything is going to be fine now.

My mother rests her hand on my shoulder. "I need you and Jalaal to keep the little ones busy while we talk."

"But I'm the reason he's here, Ammi."

Her face softens. "I know, Bilal. You took a risk, and it turned out to be a wonderful thing. Your father will be so proud of you."

Baba. I should be thinking about Baba, not about spending more time with Omar Khan.

"Okay." I look back at Jalaal, who is trying to keep Humza from picking tulips in the garden.

Ammi kisses the top of my head, then slips inside and closes the door.

Olivia comes out of her house and nods toward the sleek car with the sunglasses-wearing men inside. "What's up?"

"It's a long story," Jalaal says.

Humza trots over to Hira as she emerges from the garage with her bike.

"Do you know the game of cricket?" I ask Olivia.

She tilts her head. "I've heard of it. It's kind of like baseball?"

Jalaal and I grin. "Sort of," we both say.

I point to our house, where Omar Khan is probably telling everyone right now about his plan for helping Baba. "In that house is the world's greatest cricket player. His name is Omar Khan, and he is going to arrange for my father to come here. Finally."

Olivia's eyes go wide. "Bilal, that's great!"

"We can't go in, though." I lower my voice. "They are making a plan."

Olivia nods. "I'll just have to wait to meet him."

Humza shrieks and bursts into tears. We spin around to find him in a heap on the driveway next to Hira.

Hira's eyes fill with tears. "He wanted to sit on my bike." She sniffs.

Olivia is the first to reach Humza. She scoops him up and inspects his knee; a trickle of blood runs to his ankle. Humza takes one look at his knee and whimpers.

"I've got this," she says, then looks at Jalaal. "We've got Band-Aids at my house."

So I am left watching Hira, her purple helmet glinting in the late-afternoon sun as she rides up the sidewalk, all the way to Lizzie's driveway.

Olivia and Jalaal return with Humza just as Auntie opens the front door. When she sees Humza's knee, now cleaned up and sporting a Band-Aid, she hurries over. Humza reaches for Auntie, who smiles at Olivia, which makes Jalaal smile, too.

Omar Khan says his good-byes to Uncle and Ammi, then turns to me. He bends down so we're face-to-face. "I will do my best to help your father, Bilal."

I nod. "Thank you, sir."

"I remember him from his days on the national team. It was a shame when he had to stop playing."

So Omar Khan does remember Baba after all these years.

"Your father is a good man, and you are a brave son. I cannot guarantee anything, Bilal, but I will do my best."

One of the men in sunglasses opens the door for Omar Khan. He slides into the backseat, the doors shut, and then they're off.

Off to help Baba.

Twenty-eight

That evening Auntie calls me to the door. "Your friends are here, Bilal."

I am positive I have no friends anymore, but when I get to the door I find Henry and Akash standing on the porch. I step outside, closing the door behind me.

"Hey." And that's all I can think of to say.

Akash shifts from one foot to the other. "Hey, Bilal." He looks at Henry and then back to me. "We heard all about it—you know, throwing that ball to help your dad."

"Yeah." I sigh. "I'm sorry I lost the game."

Henry nods. "It was pretty painful to watch."

Akash elbows him, and Henry rushes to add, "At least you threw that long pitch for a reason. Jordan totally choked on the mound—she was off her game."

Akash steps forward. "I totally get it. I mean, Omar Khan!" His wide eyes make me smile, and I know he really does get it.

"If anyone can get your dad over here, it's him." He friendship-punches my shoulder. "We'll see you around, okay?"

They turn to go, and Henry mutters, "Look who's coming."

I turn to see Jordan making her way up my driveway.

"I'm outta here." Henry starts across the lawn, away from Jordan. Akash starts to follow.

"Wait," I say.

Henry turns. "What is it?"

Jordan marches up onto the porch, ignoring the guys. She puts her hands on her hips. "Jalaal says you're definitely quitting baseball."

"What?" Akash steps back up onto the porch. "Man, you can't quit the team."

Henry shakes his head. "I would give anything for a spot on the Cardinals. Don't give up yours."

Jordan folds her arms. "Look, if you hate playing, Bilal, then fine. But don't quit because of one game."

Akash chimes in. "She's right. You gave away that pitch for a good reason."

I had no idea they would even care if I quit the team.

Henry sneers at Jordan. "So what's your excuse? What happened to you out there?"

She opens her mouth to speak, then turns to go.

I haven't been a great friend to Jordan, but I can't let the guys think she doesn't deserve to be on the team. "She is worried about her dad, too."

Henry's sneer is replaced by a raised eyebrow. "Your dad?"

Jordan whirls around. "My dad has nothing to do with this."

Jordan wipes her eyes with an angry swipe of her hand. She

draws in a breath and says, "He's in Afghanistan, that's all. So are a lot of other parents. It's no big deal." She looks right at me, half daring, half pleading with me to not tell the rest of the story. And I don't; it is not my story to tell.

Akash is the first to apologize. "Sorry we've been . . ."

Jordan sniffs, but her eyes are no longer shiny. ". . . such jerks?"

Akash flashes half a grin and nods. "Yeah. Total jerks."

Henry folds his arms. "Speak for yourself."

We stare at him. He offers a sheepish grin and says, "Fine, okay. I'm sorry, too."

✦ ✦ ✦

So I go back to playing baseball, back to waiting for Baba. The month of Ramadan begins with our daily pre-dawn *suhoor* and post-sunset *iftar* meals, without Baba. Last year's start of Ramadan feels like ages ago, back when my whole life was still in Karachi. I wanted this Ramadan to be my first fasting year, to go without food or water from sunset to sundown, like a grown-up. But Ammi says that with the baseball district and state tournaments coming up, I have to break my fast after school so I'll be ready for afternoon practices.

At least I have baseball to distract me from the fact that it's been almost a year since I've seen Baba. Eleven whole months, for anyone who is counting.

I try to imagine Omar Khan talking to politicians and other important people who have strings to pull.

Now that we aren't going to Toronto, everyone is focused on the state championship finals. I play in every Cardinals game now, on the mound half the time, and Jordan pitching the other half. Since the Loudoun team will be away in Toronto on July fourth, everyone thinks we'll win this year's state championship, no problem.

A win at state won't be as sweet as it would if the Loudoun team were there to beat. But it gives us all a new goal, and sometimes just having a goal is enough to keep you swinging at all the balls that fly your way.

Jalaal and I always give Jordan a ride to practice now, and it doesn't matter if the other guys see us or not.

Today when we swing by Jordan's house to pick her up, no one answers the door.

Jalaal shrugs. "Maybe she got a ride with Coach Matt."

But when we get to the field, Jordan isn't there, and neither is Coach Matt. Practice goes on without them.

"It's probably nothing," Jalaal says on our way home.

But with the district tournament next week, Coach Matt himself said no one was allowed to miss practice.

When we pass Jordan's house on our way home, something is different.

"Stop the car!" I'm already reaching to unbuckle my seat belt.

"Whoa—hold on, little buddy." Jalaal pulls over and parks.

When I jump out of the car, Jalaal calls, "Wait up!"

I stop short, but not because Jalaal told me to wait.

"What is it, Bilal?" Jalaal's door slams.

I point to the towering tree and its bare trunk. "The yellow ribbon—it's gone."

We stand there for a few moments, staring at the ribbon-less tree trunk. Why would Jordan take it down?

Jalaal slips his phone from his back pocket. "I'm texting

Coach Matt." His thumbs fly over the screen as he mumbles, "At your house. No one home. All okay?" We watch the screen, waiting for the ping of a text from Coach Matt.

The text never comes, but Coach Matt does, around the side yard. "Hey, guys!" His smile is contagious.

He claps Jalaal on the shoulder. "My brother-in-law is back."

Just as I'm trying to figure out if a brother-in-law is the same thing as a brother, Jordan comes jogging over.

"Hey!" She stops in front of us, grinning. "My dad's here." She takes in a deep breath and lets it out in a whoosh. "He surprised me!"

Coach Matt heads back toward the side yard and waves for us to follow. "You guys hungry? Come on out back."

Jalaal and I glance at each other and follow them around to the backyard. Since it's still the month of Ramadan, we're supposed to wait until after sunset to eat dinner with our family.

"I'll introduce you to my dad!" I have never seen Jordan smile with her whole face before.

In the backyard, Coach Matt flips a hamburger on the grill, and a lady who must be Mrs. Coach Matt comes out with a pitcher of iced tea. Jordan's mom looks up from the table, where she's arranging napkins and forks on a red, white, and blue tablecloth. She smiles when she sees us.

Jordan skips over to her father, who's seated in a wooden deck chair. Next to him, leaning on the deck railing, are a pair of crutches. He looks thinner than I remember from the time I saw him at the Holiday Sing-Along. But that only makes him look more like Jordan.

Jordan beams. "Jalaal, this is my dad." Her eyes shine, and I can't help but smile, too. "And this is Bilal."

Jalaal shakes his hand first. "Welcome home, sir."

I shake his hand next, and he says, "Jordan's told me about that left arm of yours. She's grateful you're both on the same team so she doesn't have to go up against that pitching arm."

Jordan's cheeks flush red. "Dad . . ." She rolls her eyes.

"Thank you, sir."

"You two are welcome to stay and eat, if you'd like."

Coach Matt closes the grill lid. "I've got more burgers back in the kitchen. I can put them on anytime."

"Thank you," Jalaal says, "but we've got dinner waiting at home."

We say our good-byes, and Jordan walks us around to the front yard.

Jalaal heads for the car, but I wait back with Jordan for a minute.

"That's great your father is home."

She bends down and plucks a white, fuzzy dandelion from the grass. "It was a total surprise."

I try to imagine what that must have been like—seeing her father again after all this time and knowing now that he's going to be okay.

Jalaal waves from the car window. "Let's roll, little buddy."

I turn to go.

"Bilal."

I stop.

"Your dad will come back, too."

I want to say thank you, but the words are lodged in my chest. Jordan must know this, because when I look back, she's already walking away.

Jalaal must know, too; although he looks over at me a few

times, he doesn't say a word all the way home. I pick at the seams of my baseball glove and wonder if Baba will ever see me play. Is Omar Khan even trying to help Baba? If so, it's not working.

We pull into our driveway, and Jalaal is the first out of the car. He stops, his door still open.

"Hey, little buddy," he says softly. "Come see this."

I get out of the car. There, tied around the trunk of our tree, is the faded yellow ribbon.

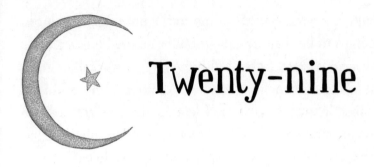

Twenty-nine

We win the district championship, seven to two. Next stop—state finals in a town called McLean, only twenty minutes away. It's no Toronto, but if we win the state title, we get to play in a place called Georgia.

We've got one week left of fifth grade. Mrs. Wu says middle school will open our worlds to new opportunities—clubs and elective classes and new friends. We'll have lockers with combination locks, seven different teachers, PE uniforms and locker rooms, and a library filled to bursting with books just for older kids—us.

Akash dumps his backpack on the bus seat in front of me and opens his window. "Want to hit the pool after practice?"

"Did someone say *pool*? I'm in." Henry plops down next to me. "You coming, Bilal?"

I shake my head. "Jalaal's going to the prom, and my mom says we have to be there to take pictures before he goes."

Jordan takes the seat behind Henry. "Olivia's really nice."

I nod. I couldn't believe it when Auntie said he could go. Jalaal claims they're only going as friends and will be at the dance with a big group, so maybe that's how he convinced her. I think Humza's Band-Aid may have had something to do with it, too.

Instead of driving me to practice, Jalaal is out picking up flowers for Olivia, so Jordan's dad drives us. He can't bend his left leg very well, but he says he only needs his right leg for driving anyway.

Even though this is only a practice and not a real game, Jordan keeps glancing at her dad on the bleachers, like she wants to make sure he's still there. Every time she does, he gives her a smile. And every time that happens, my heart swells and breaks at the same time.

"He's not going back, you know," Jordan says as we jog out toward Coach Pablo for pitching practice. "He's looking for a different job now."

It never occurred to me that Jordan might move away now that her dad is back. "A job where—back in Illinois?"

She shakes her head. "Around here, where we're close to family."

I smile.

"And friends." She friendship-punches my shoulder.

✦ ✦ ✦

I have never seen Jalaal this nervous. Auntie straightens his seafoam green bow tie. Uncle checks the battery level on the camera. Hira opens the refrigerator and takes out the plastic box containing Olivia's flowers, holding it like it's made of glass. Ammi keeps Humza and his yogurt-covered fingers away from Jalaal's black tuxedo. I'm in charge of the iPad as we Skype with Baba, Daddo, and everyone else back in Karachi. I pan around the room before zooming in on Jalaal as Auntie smooths the lapels of his jacket. She turns him toward the camera and smiles. Applause and a murmur of approval come from the iPad, which I can't see since I'm the one filming.

"Okay." Jalaal takes a deep breath. "I'm heading out."

Auntie hands him the plastic box with Olivia's flowers. "We're coming with you."

Panic flashes across Jalaal's face until Auntie grins and says, "Only outside to take pictures."

Jalaal lets out a breath and kisses Auntie on the cheek.

We trail behind Jalaal out the front door, with the Karachi relatives and me bringing up the rear.

Hira points to the teenagers and parents standing in Olivia's driveway. "Look!" She squeals and covers her mouth. "They're so fancy!"

Jalaal looks like he'd rather not have our family parade outside with him, but his face changes completely when he sees Olivia. They walk toward each other, grinning. They don't even notice when I zoom in on their faces with the iPad.

Now I get why Jalaal's bow tie is seafoam green—it matches Olivia's flowy dress.

Hira claps. "Olivia's a princess!"

We laugh, and Jalaal says, "Agreed."

"What's going on?" Daddo's voice comes from the iPad. I translate what Hira said about Olivia being a princess, and they

233

all murmur and nod. Daddo's eyes are shiny as she blows a kiss. Jalaal and Olivia wave into the camera, and the relatives wave back and talk at once. Jalaal tells them he wishes they were here with us, and Daddo shakes her head and clasps her hands together, her eyes smiling.

Olivia watches in awe as Jalaal speaks in Urdu, like he's some kind of genius.

We join the other families on Olivia's front lawn for pictures of all the prom couples. Then the other teenagers climb into a long car called a *limo*, even nicer than Omar Khan's car. Jalaal and Olivia get into our car because they aren't going straight to dinner. Since it's still Ramadan and Jalaal needs to wait for sundown to eat, Olivia suggested they take a walk in DC near the monuments while they wait for the sun to set. Then they'll eat at some famous restaurant at the very top of a tall building. After dessert, they will join their friends at the dance.

Jalaal drives past us, giving a honk, and we wave. The adults stay out on Olivia's lawn, talking and laughing and shaking their heads when someone says something about how fast kids grow up. I bring the Karachi relatives inside for now, and they all sign off except for Baba.

"Bilal *jaan*, I have another Karachi memory for you." Baba smiles. "Remember the rickshaws?"

"Yes, Baba—I almost forgot! I have not seen a single one here."

"I think that Jalaal and Olivia should have taken a rickshaw ride to their dance."

Baba and I laugh picturing Jalaal and Olivia all dressed up, squished into an open rickshaw cab pulled by a loud, stinky motor scooter.

234

"Now it's your turn, Bilal. What American tidbit do you have for me?" Baba's smile is still wide, but I can feel mine starting to fade.

There are lots of things I could tell Baba, like how the pools are open again or how I took my end-of-year school exams on a computer. I could tell him about the giant elephant statue I saw on our museum field trip to DC or the tornado drill we had at school.

"Bilal?" Baba's smile is gone. "Are you all right?"

I shrug. "I can't think of any more American things for your list, Baba."

Because he needs to come and see America for himself. I don't say this, but looking at his face, I can tell Baba agrees.

Thirty

"How would you like to celebrate your birthday, Bilal?" Ammi sits at the kitchen table, a pen poised above a clean pad of paper. "We can invite your friends over, go to the pool—whatever you'd like."

She writes *Bilal's 11th birthday* and underlines it twice. "Of course, your big game is at noon that day, but your friends can come over afterward—maybe for fireworks that evening?"

I slump into the chair across from her. "I don't really feel like celebrating this year."

She sets her pen down. "I know, Bilal."

And that's all she needs to say.

All the summer birthdays are announced on the last day of school, so people know I'll be eleven soon. Jordan and the guys ask what I'm doing for my birthday, but I tell them I haven't decided yet. Hopefully they'll forget and stop asking.

These last days of Ramadan feel different this year. On last year's Eid, we thought Baba would be joining us soon. This year, it feels like he never will. Maybe Omar Khan's connections didn't work. Maybe not even the world's greatest cricket player can get Baba here.

Auntie, Ammi, and Hira get swirly henna designs on their hands, and I go to the batting cages whenever I can. There's only a week and a half left before the state championship game, but Coach Matt and Coach Pablo give us Sunday off, just in time for Eid.

When the holiday arrives, after the pre-dawn morning prayer, I wish everyone *Eid Mubarak*. I hug each of them three times, then crawl back into bed. I want this day to be over.

Ammi comes in as the morning light begins to glow behind my window shade. She sits on the edge of my bed, then touches my forehead and rests her hand for a moment on my cheek.

"Are you hungry, Bilal *jaan*? *Suhoor* is on the table."

I shake my head. I used to love the pre-dawn meal, where everyone starts off hungry and sleepy and ends up full and happy.

Ammi sighs and adjusts my covers like she used to when she tucked me in for the night. "Oh, Bilal." Her voice catches, and she presses her fingers to her mouth. The festive henna swirls across her hand seem lost, out of place. Baba always loved to see which design Ammi and Hira would choose on Chaand Raat, the Night of the Moon right before Eid. Baba would trace the lines on Hira's hands until she couldn't hold her giggles in any longer.

I reach for Ammi's hand, and she gives mine a squeeze.

Sometimes I forget that I am not the only one who misses Baba.

I get up, not because I want to, but because this makes Ammi smile, her eyes bright with tears.

I get through it all—prayers at the mosque, visiting friends, and eating pounds of *sheer khorma*. After the second house, I've already had enough of the creamy milk pudding.

When it is time to Skype with the family back in Karachi, Hira actually lets Humza steal the show with his big, wet kisses right on the screen. Everyone applauds on the Karachi side, while Hira whispers, "Ew." She doesn't try to elbow her way into the conversation like she used to, and I know it's because she's losing more and more Urdu words.

I get through more prayers, the dinner feast, the gifts, and finally I am back in bed. I don't dream about the next Eid. In fact, I don't have any dreams at all.

✦   ✦   ✦

In the week leading up to the tournament, I run my fastest and swing my hardest. When I'm on the pitching mound, everyone says I'm on fire, including Jordan.

Sunday we have another day off, and I don't know what to do with myself. The tournament is in two days, and it feels like it will never get here. Just like Baba.

Everyone is busy except for me. Even Jordan is away for the day with her family. Jalaal is hardly around anymore since he got a summer job at the nursery and garden center with Olivia.

Uncle has errands to run. Ammi and Auntie haven't stopped cooking all morning, and Hira chases Humza around the backyard.

Telling Ammi I'm bored turns out to be a big mistake. I have to set the table even though dinner isn't for hours, then sweep the garage and pull weeds from the flower bed out back.

Finally Ammi calls me inside to wash up.

Jalaal is already back from the nursery, and he gets to the shower first.

Auntie announces that since summer has now arrived, all of us should read. "Every day for thirty minutes—adults, too," Auntie says, beaming like this is the world's all-time greatest idea.

Hira actually does think it's a great idea. Jalaal looks less thrilled, but he cheers up when Auntie says he can download a baseball book. I would volunteer to read to Humza, but he's taking a nap. Ammi flips through a magazine too fast to read anything, and I wonder if just looking at the pictures counts. What am I going to read?

Then I remember my issues of *Sports Illustrated Kids*, so I bring a stack into the living room. I flip to the table of contents and sigh. There are no articles on cricket.

I hear Uncle's car pull up, and I wonder if he knows about Auntie's new summer reading plan. He'd better have something to read. He hasn't come through the door yet, and I almost wish I could warn him.

And then I hear it.

Two fast raps on the door—pause—another quick knock like a hiccup, followed by two slow thunks.

Baba's special knock.

My head snaps up, not daring to believe. I look at Ammi, who smiles through tears. She nods. "Go, Bilal."

I scramble to my feet and race down the hall.

There are no locks to undo, not like last time; I fling the door open.

There, standing on the porch, is Baba.

I throw my arms around him and he laughs, swinging me off my feet. All the things I thought I'd forgotten come back in an instant—Baba's strong arms, the way his laughter sounds in my ear, the smell of cologne on his collar.

The stampede in the hallway announces the arrival of everyone else, and there are hugs and tears and more hugs. Baba and Ammi look at each other like they are seeing a lost treasure found.

Baba is home.

 # Thirty-one

Baba doesn't talk about the days when he went missing, at least not to me. But he does talk about the day he got the news that he was coming to us at last.

"It was because of you, Bilal." His eyes still shine when he smiles, just like I remember.

"My friend Jack says politicians can pull strings."

Baba smiles. "Omar Khan did not just pull strings, he cut right through them as if they were threads from a spider web."

Baba and I laugh, and it is the most beautiful sound I have ever heard.

Baba unzips his suitcase and takes something from the side pocket that crinkles. "From Daddo." He holds up a familiar purple packet with the dancing chili peppers on the front.

"Chili Milis!"

He tosses me the spicy gummy candies shaped like peppers, and I rip open the bag.

"Daddo remembers how much you love these."

I put one Chili Mili in my mouth and chew, my eyes watering at the spicy kick. I wish I could thank Daddo in person. I roll the bag closed and promise myself that I will only eat one a day to make them last.

"Will Daddo ever come to live with us here in America one day?"

Baba sits on the bed, next to his suitcase. "No, Bilal. As much as she loves us, she wants to stay in her home and in Karachi with the rest of the family."

"Can she visit?"

Baba nods. "I have no doubt that she will."

Maybe I should start a list of things to know about America for Daddo when she comes.

I ask Baba about Mudassar.

Baba nods like he knew this question was coming. "Mudassar could use a good friend like you right about now."

I frown. "His father?"

Baba rubs his face with his hands before looking me in the eye. "His father has gone to prison, Bilal *jaan*."

I would think Baba would be relieved about this; now he doesn't have to worry that he'll be blamed for what Mudassar's father did. But Baba only looks sad.

I will call Mudassar. But first I need time to catch up with Baba and show him all the things that he's missed here in America.

I open my desk drawer and take out my list of things for Baba to know about America. Baba laughs and takes out his list, too. We pin them side by side on my bulletin board.

"Close your eyes, Bilal *jaan*, and hold out your hands."

I hear Baba rise from the bed and rummage through his suitcase.

Then I feel it. My fingers close around the smooth wood, and even with my eyes closed, I know there is nothing else it could be—my cricket bat.

I run my fingers over the signatures of my faraway friends—Karachi Youth Tournament champions, every one of us. My bat took up suitcase space that Baba could have used for other things. "Baba—thank you."

My father smiles. "I promised, didn't I?"

I nod, my heart so full I cannot speak.

"And one more thing." He reaches into his carry-on bag and pulls out a cricket ball.

I grin. "Now we can teach Jalaal to play."

Baba laughs. "Perhaps not with this."

He turns the ball, revealing something scrawled in permanent marker:

For Bilal the Brave
Your friend,
Omar Khan

I gape at the ball, at this gift from the great Omar Khan. And then I hug Baba, because he is the real gift.

✦ ✦ ✦

I thought I would be nervous to have Baba watch me play baseball. Although I have improved so much in one year, I am still not as good at baseball as I once was at cricket.

For the state championship game, I would like to say I struck out more batters than Jordan did. I would like to say I made it past second base. I would like to say I was the star of the game. I was not. My whole team was the star of that game, because together we beat the Williamsburg Wombats, seven to six. Baba says it's the most exciting game he has ever seen in his entire life.

My favorite part wasn't when I struck out two batters, or when I made it to second base with one hit. The best part was when I took the mound and saw Baba there in the stands. When he patted his heart twice, I patted mine twice, too. It wasn't for luck; it was his way of saying, "I love watching you play baseball," and it was my way of saying back, "Thank you for being here."

That evening, we celebrate the Cardinals' win, America's birthday, and my birthday all rolled into one. Neighborhood friends come by for food and to watch the fireworks from the high school. I introduce Baba to Jordan and her family, who all say, "Welcome to America!" Baba shakes hands with Akash and Henry. Jordan unties the yellow ribbon, and together we put it in the trash can.

This year I don't sit in a lawn chair with the grown-ups; I run and whoop and laugh with my friends as pinpoint lights soar skyward, burst, and fall back to earth.

Right before the big fireworks finale, everyone sings "Happy Birthday" to me, and Baba's voice is as loud as Hira's.

Jalaal points as the final rockets of light rise into the night and join the stars high above us before exploding into a hundred colors—the best birthday candle I have ever had. Last year I made a wish on my birthday; this year I don't need to.

The sparks wink themselves out as they float back down, and everyone claps at the grand finale. For my family, though, this is our grand beginning. I have decided that sometimes America means mom, baseball, and apple pie; sometimes it means Baba, cricket, and *jalebi*.

Baba once said the fourth of July would be the best day of my life.

He is right.

Acknowledgments

This book would not exist without the input and encouragement from a whole team of folks. My thanks begin with my agent, Erin Murphy, who encouraged me to write a proposal for this story. When it sold to Charlesbridge, my giddiness over selling three chapters and a synopsis quickly turned to mild panic as the reality of crafting an entire novel set in. All of a sudden I had deadlines, which were set (and, mercifully, revised) by my editor, Julie Bliven. I first met this novel's main character, Bilal, in a handful of scenes from my first novel, *Flying the Dragon*. In that story, he was a minor character, but I knew he had his own story to tell. Thanks to Julie's support, guidance, and encouragement, I found the space and the inspiration I needed to delve into Bilal's world. I also appreciate

Emily Mitchell's proofreading prowess, Diane Earley's diligence with this book's design, and copyeditor Josette Haddad's knowledge of baseball (among a multitude of other topics) that helped wrangle some of this story's details into line. I am so grateful for Kelly Murphy, artist extraordinaire, whose talent has graced yet another children's-book cover.

Regarding all things baseball, I'd like to thank Nate Contrino, Harry Fulton, Carter Strain, and my dad, Chuck Dias, who has been a die-hard Red Sox fan for the last seventy-something years. Any inaccuracies that may remain are mine alone. Regarding all things cricket, I decided to change the names of the professional cricket players mentioned in this story, since these characters are based on real people who are still living.

I can't imagine writing a book without the insight, encouragement, and honest feedback from my long-time critique partners Joan Paquette, Julie Phillipps, and Kip Wilson. My mother, Carol Dias, also read through the manuscript and helped keep this story on track.

I never would have been able to write this book without the help of friends who have a close connection to Pakistani and Pakistani American culture. Fellow author and friend Hena Khan read through this manuscript several times and offered invaluable insights, even emailing relatives back in Pakistan to find answers to my questions. Fahd Patel, attorney by day and first-time dad by night, was kind enough to reply to an email from a stranger after I stumbled across a *Zindagi 360* interview where he talked about his Pakistani American experience. His wife, Sahar Khan, generously provided answers to questions that I didn't even know I had and read through the manuscript, all while working on her PhD and raising a baby son. My former colleague, Sughra Kolia, is not only a wonderful teacher, but also a kind friend who shared tidbits of her life here in the US and in Karachi. My thanks to Amrita Love and Shaziya Ali, who are sweeter than jalebi.

My students have inspired my writing more than they will ever know. One of my many, many wishes for them is that they will one day tell their own stories from their own unique world experiences. I hope that my students and all readers will follow the good work behind We Need Diverse Books, an organization that helps people of all ages find and value their own stories.

My biggest thanks go to Davide, who gives me the encouragement and time to write; Teah, who always knows when I need a latte break; Sofia, who offered her own insights on the manuscript; and Jordan, who let me use his name for a baseball-playing girl. I am so very lucky to have you all on my team.